Tyrean Martinson

25 IMPOSSIBLE TALES OF SURVIVORS, FLAWED HEROES, AND ANNOYED VILLAINS

25 IMPOSSIBLE TALES

OF SURVIVORS, FLAWED HEROES, AND ANNOYED VILLAINS: A Science Fiction and Fantasy Collection

Tyrean Martinson

Contents

Intro ... VII

1. HELP WANTED: CODE GRAY ... 1

2. SHADOW MAGIC ... 6

3. THE BLADE SMITH OF BRIN ... 17

4. WAKING UP ALIEN ... 26

5. THE GREAT ELEVATOR ... 31

6. ROOT DEEP ... 39

7. WISHES ... 43

8. HEARING THINGS ... 47

9. NEW ANSWERS ... 49

10. LIFE POD ... 56

11. 11:06 THE TIME OF NOW ... 61

12. KARRN SURVIVAL ... 65

13. OF CLONES AND ROBOPUPPIES ... 69

14. WHEN LIFE IS ALMOST AS STRANGE AS FICTION   76

15. DEAR DREAD LORD   83

16. HOTHOUSE   86

17. THE SHIMMER   97

18. HERE THERE BE DRAGONS!   102

19. TRUST AND LIES   111

20. AM I A MONSTER?   115

21. OUT OF MANY, ONE   123

22. NEW AND OLD HORIZONS   125

23. OF WORDS AND SWORDS   131

24. ENOUGH TO DO   151

25. A COMPANION FOR THE JOURNEY   156

PREVIOUS PUBLICATIONS   161

NOTES ON STORIES   163

ABOUT THE AUTHOR   171

MORE TO READ!   173

Intro

Speculative fiction can range from the outright, noticeably hard sci-fi and all-encompassing fantasy worlds to the somewhat subtle supernatural and sci-fi elements like those we see in the Indiana Jones movies.

The genre offers us a wonderfully, flexible landscape with blurry edges in which to ask tough questions about humanity and morality, go play in a field of unicorns and leprechauns, or attempt to do all of those. We can read *The Hitchiker's Guide to the Galaxy, Lord of the Rings, The Stand,* and *The Last Unicorn,* and still be within the huge, welcoming space of speculative fiction.

In speculative fiction, we get to ask questions. What will someone do when faced with completely impossible odds? Calculate them like C-3PO, go full speed like Han Solo, get one with the force like Luke, attempt diplomacy like Leia? Or put shields on full and attempt diplomacy first with fingers ready on defensive weapons' arrays like in many *Star Trek* scenarios?

Will the characters fight for survival and freedom or give into despair (*Hunger Games*), and if they fight, is there a right way and a wrong way, and who determines that? Can the characters beat the insurmountable odds, or is it too late (*Divergent and 1984*)? What makes us human, and can AI be "human" in the way we mean? (*Blade Runner*)

With those questions and more in mind, I assembled speculative fiction short stories I've written mostly over the last six years into this new book: 25 Impossible Tales of Survivors, Flawed Heroes, and Annoyed Villains, A Science Fiction and Fantasy Collection.

No matter how hard circumstances are, there is hope for survival, even if it means making one simple choice in the right direction or standing up in the face of impossible odds. But the question remains: What is the right direction and which way is up?

**The main text of this introduction came from an answer to a question for the Insecure Writer's Support Group monthly blog hop. The question was: What do you consider the best characteristics of your favorite genre?*

HELP WANTED: CODE GRAY

Dave felt a headache coming on as soon as he opened the first of the virtual classifieds. He needed a job. Everyone wanted experience. The best jobs were taken by the time he clicked through and the worst ones wouldn't even hire him because he didn't have "expertise" in their particular field of horse manure.

A sip of his coffee eased the ache in his sore throat but did nothing for his stuffed nasal passages. In addition to being out of work, he was sick. Even if the perfect job opening landed in his lap, he'd probably sneeze all over his future employers. Definitely not a good idea these days. And how would he interview in a mask? He glanced down at his gray tie and suit jacket.

A few weeks ago, his suit jacket had been fashionably tight, and now it easily overlapped. His mother would cluck over his skinny frame if she saw him, but he didn't want to give his older brother the satisfaction of proving his predictions about him right if he showed up home after college with no job and giant loans riding his shoulders.

Dave sighed again. None of his family angst was putting money in his pocket. His drip coffee kept him out of the fall chill, but it wouldn't last long. He had just enough money in his accounts to keep him from the streets for another few weeks. Or, he could buy a bus ticket home.

No, he told himself. He would do anything other than go home with his tail between his legs. He sat up straight, trying to use his posture to improve his mood as he glanced out the window in time to see a classified ad flash on the billboard across the street.

"Help Wanted: Apply in Person by Midnight. Gray Building, Suite 42. Code: Gray."

Dave closed his eyes for a moment, wondering if he was going a little crazy. When he opened his eyes again, the ad flashed across the billboard and paused there.

The choice didn't seem like a choice at all. Even if he had no idea what kind of job it was, Dave felt desperate enough to check it out. With one last dab at his nose, he gathered his things, then took three more napkins from the dispenser and shoved them in his pocket.

Outside the coffee shop, he walked briskly to the Gray building. It loomed above him, completely concrete except for the top floor of windows that winked in the chilly autumn sunlight. The doors, which always looked un-inviting, were closed

Dave felt a thrill of nervousness run through him. He remembered joking with his college buddies that the Gray building was actually a morgue of epic proportions – a place where all the bodies were hidden, when the government wanted to cover something up. They had laughed about it, thinking it was a clever sort of thing to say. Now, it didn't seem clever.

The door swung open in front of him, and a young woman with a brilliant tangle of shimmery afro-curls stepped out and walked towards him.

"We've been expecting you," she said.

"Uh." Dave felt transfixed by fear and interest.

"Don't you want to apply for the job?" She cocked an eyebrow at him, and put her manicured hands on her hips. She was dressed in a charcoal gray pant-suit that hugged her curves and flared out at the ankles.

"Sure," Dave heard himself say. He felt like he'd gotten lost in a fog as he followed her into the building.

Inside, the walls were all dark gray, and even the decorations – a huge fountain in the center of the atrium, and an oil painting – were in various shades of gray.

"Your interview is in Suite 42. I'll take you up." The gorgeous woman led him towards a bank of elevators, and then offered her hand. "My name's Kestral Hawk."

"Seriously?"

She raised her eyebrows.

"I mean, that's a beautiful name, but it's a . . . well, your parents must love birds."

She laughed a husky, echoing laugh that filled the whole room.

When the elevator doors opened, she walked in and pressed 42.

Dave followed her. "I'm Dave."

"I know." She smirked at him.

Dave wanted to ask how she knew, and what this was all about, and he suddenly wondered if this was some kind of prank, but the elevator rose with a jostling swiftness and then the doors swooshed open to reveal a plush, charcoal carpeted space with multiple screens stretched across the opposite walls.

Dave stepped into the room.

"Good luck, Dave."

The doors closed, Kestral Hawk was gone, and Dave was alone with a bunch of blinking screens in a large, gray office space.

The screens flared to life all at once, depicting world maps with ciphers running across the bottom. It reminded Dave of his favorite game on his notebook, the one he had been playing all the way through college. He went to the small keyboard and began to solve the ciphers, one after another, sometimes having to match them with the correct section of the world maps. He didn't know how long he worked. The room had a constant light. As he solved the last cipher, the screens went dark.

The doors of the elevator opened behind him, and Dave turned to see Kestral Hawk enter the room.

"You're hired," Kestral Hawk said.

Dave sneezed.

"Bio-signature accepted," said a computerized voice.

"But what kind of job is it?"

"The kind that lets you solve puzzles for work, pays off your loans, and isn't something you write home to mumsy about," Kestral said. "We're keeping secrets safe, Dave. It's what Grays do."

"So, this is where they hide the bodies," he said.

Kestral shrugged. "You need a job, don't you?"

"When do I start?"

"You already did, Dave."

Dave felt his stomach plummet. "What organization is this?"

"We serve the country's best interests, Dave. Don't worry. And, we'll take care of your illness before you even start." She pulled a wicked-looking syringe from her pocket and poked it through his suit jacket and into his skin before he could protest.

Dave forced himself to relax against the pain and all of the fear shooting through his mind. At least he had a job. He could figure out the rest, later.

SHADOW MAGIC

THERESE HAD JUST MANAGED to escape from her room when destiny showed up on her doorstep, several feet below her. Clinging to the branches of the sorrel tree, Therese listened as the two riders banged on the front door of her father's house. They hadn't even bothered dismounting and one of the horses had flecks of sweat in its mane.

Finally, the door creaked open and Therese's stepmother confronted the riders. "What do you mean by . . . oh, I apologize for my manner, Lords. I thought that ruffians had . . ."

"Never mind that, good woman. May we speak to Master Chutney?"

Therese's stepmother put her hand to her chest and shook her head sorrowfully, "ah, my Clement. He died only a fortnight ago and . . ."

"Did he have any heirs?"

"Excuse me?" Therese's stepmother lost her sorrowful act.

The second rider, a woman, put up her hand. "We mean no offense, Mistress Chutney, but our errand is urgent. We need the heir of Master Chutney for a rite at Shadow Castle."

"Well, now, my husband passed without any male heirs, but he did have a daughter, a sickly child with . . ."

In her tree, Therese stiffened. She wasn't sickly. She was house-bound by her step-mother, forced to do indoor chores and never let out of the attic, except by escape.

The horsewoman glanced upward and caught sight of Therese in the tree. "Why don't you come down, girl? And, come with us. We have need of you in a life and death situation."

Therese clung to the bark, willing herself to blend. She wasn't sure she wanted to take part in any rite at Shadow Castle. Her father hadn't liked the wizards there, often crossing the street to get away from them in the market and muttering about how he couldn't stand the sight of them in church.

Fading didn't work. She supposed it was too late now that the riders had noticed her.

"Therese! Get down here, now!" Therese's stepmother bellowed up at her, and then turned sweetly to the horse riders. "I'm so sorry, but she gets these addled thoughts in her sickly head, and I really don't think a rite at the Shadow Castle would . . ."

"How much?" asked the woman.

"What? I can't think what you might . . ."

"How much money do you want for her, to take her off of your hands?" the woman stated.

The male horse-rider had reined his horse backwards, slightly. He looked up at Therese.

As she looked at his black eyes, Therese didn't feel the chill her father warned her about; but she did feel a longing. She scrambled down the tree and went to stand by his stirrup, staring up at his dark eyes.

"That's enough, Reggie."

The man, Reggie, blinked, and suddenly his eyes were a muddy brown.

Therese backed away from him. "How? Why?"

"We didn't have time to do this gently, child," the woman said.

"I'm no child!" Therese stood up straight and glared at the woman. She was an adult, short for her age, but an adult.

"Good and I'm Daria, of the First Order. We need your help to unlock the scrolls of the Wizard Chutney, of the 7th order."

"There's never been a wizard in the Chutney family."

Daria sighed. "I wish that were true, considering your family's streak of stubbornness. Now, we haven't time to waste. Get on the back of my horse, and you might just have a chance to save a life."

Therese didn't particularly want to ride on the back of the woman's mare, but she didn't want to stay with her stepmother either. This was, at least, a chance for freedom. She accepted the woman's help and swung up behind her saddle, sitting on the edge of blanket behind it.

They rode in silence. Therese had the sense to see that the other two were grim and hurried. For her part, she thought she should study them more closely before she submitted to some rite at Shadow castle and helped them unlock scrolls, if she even could.

Daria's hair was tightly woven into tiny braids, which were braided together and knotted at the base of her skull. Her clothes were fitting, severe black, and well-kept. Even the tack of her horse looked like it had been polished.

Reggie, although he wore the same uniform, had a much different demeanor. His clothes looked well-worn, his boots were polished but scuffed, and the tack of his horse needed mending on the back of his saddle. Despite all of this, he sat straight and rode just as well as Daria.

Therese wasn't sure what to make of either of them by the time that the towers of Shadow Keep loomed above them.

As they neared the gate, she shifted in her seat, considering the possibility of jumping off and making a run for it. She knew she couldn't outrun the horses, but the idea of going into the keep that her father had cursed so often made her twitchy.

Daria glanced back. "We need you, Therese. I wouldn't ask you, otherwise."

Therese sighed. She didn't doubt the sincerity of Daria's words. The woman seemed too intent, as if she bore a heavy weight of responsibility on her shoulders.

As they crossed through the gated threshold into the yard of Shadow Keep, Therese expected something to happen, some foreboding or prickling, or sense of unease. Instead, she felt as if she had come home.

Around them, children, young people, and elderly people were gathered around the courtyard, either cooling down horses, herding sheep into a pen, making music, or just simply talking by the stall of an enterprising coffee seller. Everyone seemed comfortable with one another; although Therese could tell that everyone was somber. Even the music held the soothing tones of a lullaby or a hymn, although it was no song that Therese had ever heard.

A few feet into the courtyard, Reggie dismounted swiftly and handed his horse off to a young man who seemed to be waiting for their mounts.

Daria nodded to Therese in encouragement.

Therese swung herself to the side of the horse, using her hands as leverage, and then slid down. As her feet touched the pavement, Therese felt a hum of contentment course through her from the soles of her feet to the top of her head, and she leaned into the flank of the horse for a moment, letting it soak into her like a warm bath. Every part of her felt invigorated, and when she looked up, she noticed that the courtyard had gone quiet.

She turned slowly and noticed the play of light and shadow over the faces of everyone in the courtyard, and on the ground, stretched out around objects and buildings. A particular shaft of brightness poured from the uppermost tower of the keep, but it was sullied by a strangely pulsating shadow unlike any of the others in the courtyard.

"What is that?" she asked Daria, pointing to but not touching the pulsating shadow.

"You see it?" Daria looked shocked. "Dear heavens, I'm glad we brought you here, Therese." She jumped down from her horse, and grabbed Therese's elbow. "Come with me now. If you can see it, then you can certainly help us defeat it."

"But it is a shadow and is this not Shadow Keep?" Therese resisted Daria's gentle pull on her arm.

"There are shadows and there are shadows," Daria said with her mouth thinned into a narrow line. "We don't work with that kind here."

Therese nodded and allowed Daria to pull her forward into the keep's castle proper. They hurried past guards, groups of students and magicians, up a grand staircase and then up a smaller spiral staircase that led upward to that small tower above. On the way, Therese would have liked to watch the shadows and the light flickers on the walls, but she could feel that pulsating miasma now, all around them, and she understood Daria's hurry.

At the top of the stairs, Daria pushed her way through another set of guarded doors, and led Therese to a book on one side of the room. The center of the room held a chair with a single occupant, whose eyes were widened in horror at the dark miasma around him. In a silent scream, he looked frozen by the darkness, but his eyes darted wildly from side to side as if searching for something.

Therese hesitated, looking at him. How was she, a mere girl from the village, supposed to save him, when he was obviously a shadow master by the cut of his clothes?

"Don't focus on him," Daria said. "This book is the one we need you to open."

Puzzled, Therese gazed at the book that Daria held in her arms. It was a thick, aged tome with a leather binding and yellowed pages.

"Why do you need me to open a book?"

"We believe it holds the cure for the mess that Roger's let loose on himself and the keep, but we can't open it. Only the true heir of the Chutney clan can do that."

"How?" Therese had heard some horrible stories about how the Shadow Magicians went about their business.

"Just stand by the window, so the light from the sun casts your shadow on the book."

"That's all? No sacrificial blood?"

Daria shook her head. "The stories they tell in the village are . . . ridiculous. No, we don't need any blood. Just your shadow."

Therese walked over to her, took the weighty book into her hands, and stood by the window so that the sun's warmth hit her face and cast her shadow on the cover of the book. Then, she opened the book's cover gently and peered inside. The pages were blank.

Therese glanced at Daria. "I don't understand."

Daria bit her lips. "Do you have a family talisman: a necklace, a charm, a pair of special glasses, a coin, or something that your father kept apart from all other things?"

Therese put her hand to her waist, just above where she kept her hidden pocket inside her clothes. It was there, but she didn't want to give it to anyone, for any reason.

"What do you have?" Daria's eyes went to Therese's hand.

"It's my family heirloom. It's one of only things I have left of my father that my stepmother hasn't taken from me."

Daria stepped back. "It's all right. I don't expect you to hand it to me, but I suggest you take it out, and cast its shadow on the book's pages. I believe it will help us to read what is hidden there."

Therese handed the book to Daria, and deftly pulled out her father's compass. For the first time, she noticed the way the light sparkled over the glass and the needle cast a shadow in different directions, based on how she held it in the sunlight. She wondered what that could mean, but she took the book from Daria's hands and cast the compass shadow over the pages. Words slowly appeared on the page, only in the shadow of the compass.

"Oh, thank the Lord of light!" Daria exclaimed. "Can you find the spell of banishment?"

Therese glanced at her, and then slowly looked over the first pages of the book, which seemed to be a neatly written table of contents. She found the title of the spell of banishment with a page number and followed that to the page she needed. "It is here," she said, showing the book to Daria.

"Please read it," Daria said.

"But aren't you the magician?"

Daria smiled. "No more than you, Therese. This is your family's magic. Please, read the spell aloud."

Therese let Daria's words sink in. She didn't want to be a magician. But, the book had opened for her. And the keep felt like home to her. And the boy in the chair was in pain. She couldn't leave him like that. So, slowly, she read the words on the page letting each one fill up the room before letting it go. It felt like the words were bits of light pouring out in to the room, and the dark miasma responded to them; first, by swelling, and finally, but slowly, diminishing into a small spot that disappeared with an audible pop.

The boy's eyes stopped darting from side to side and his gaze came to rest on Therese. "Thank you." He tried to sit up and Daria went to him, putting her arm around his shoulders.

"Take it easy, Master Roger. You're going to feel weak for some time."

He nodded, and then he held out his hand to Therese. "Please, heir of Chutney, may I know your name, now that you have come to your rightful place in Shadow Keep?"

Therese stiffened, and nearly dropped the book. Belatedly, she remembered the manners her father taught her. She folded the top of the compass and tucked it inside one hand, closed the book, and then curtseyed awkwardly in her pants. "Master Roger, I'm afraid that I must know more before I can commit to a life here."

"Of course," he said, dropping his hand. "It's not exactly a promising place when the Lord of the Castle is caught up in his own foolish mistakes and nearly pulls the keep down around everyone's ears. I'll ask Daria and some others to show you around, you can spend the night here in one of the guest rooms, and if you will break your fast with me tomorrow, we can discuss the possibilities of life here at the keep. It may be that I need a Chutney heir to keep me in line."

Daria gave Therese a glare. "You want to go back to your stepmother and let her treat you like an imbecile?"

"No," Therese said. "I'm just considering my options carefully."

Roger smiled at her. "See, that's just the kind of sense I obviously need to have around me."

Daria scowled at him. "As if all of your senior advisors didn't warn you about messing with that minor shadow demon. There's no such thing as minor shadow demons. And, although I want Therese to stay, you must know from history that the Chutneys were never known for sense, just as your line isn't."

Roger smiled. "And now, my master plan is revealed. I need someone here that will shake things up a bit." He winked at Therese.

Therese fought a smile building up her face, and she hastily hid her lips with the hand that held the compass.

When the compass passed her lips, with the sun against her profile, the shadow on the ground revealed something Therese had only seen once before in her dreams: a laughing girl standing in front of the family crest: a compass and a telescope. She stared at it, transfixed by her childhood hopes.

"What is it? What do you see?" Daria asked.

"An answer." Therese kissed the compass, and tucked it back into her pocket, where it nestled against the miniature telescope her father had given her as a child.

THE BLADE SMITH OF BRIN

I HAVE NEVER BEEN a hero. No matter what stories you've heard.

No, I don't have time to regale you with those tales. It's time for the young to get some sleep.

What will I be doing?

The forge is always best after dark. The cool night air relieves the sweltering heat of the forge, and, at the right hour, the metal is at its best.

I know you want to learn, but it isn't time, not yet. Don't worry. Your time will come.

You must have a story? All right. Just one and a tiny cup of water, not too much. And, your Izzy Warrior Doll. Yes, here it is.

Now, you're ready? Good.

Once upon a time, a young woman with fiery red hair ... Yes, like your Izzy and you.

Once upon a time, this young woman with fiery red hair imagined she would be the most gloriously good warrior the ten kingdoms had ever seen. She would rid the world of dragons and other fell beasts, win wars against the evil enemies of her land, and gain the hand of a sweet, and kind, prince.

What about handsome? Not all princes are handsome, and the kind ones are far better than the pretty ones. I know you don't understand that yet, but some day you will. Someday, too soon, I fear. No, I'm not explaining what I mean by that, not yet.

Back to the story. When the young warrior woman with fiery red hair, we'll call her Scarlet for the sake of the story, when Scarlet rode out on her mighty steed to make her fortune, she didn't know the adventures she would have. There were many good adventures, many hard adventures, but the one I'm going to tell you about tonight, it was the most unexpected, the one that changed her life forever.

Scarlet received a request from a King with sons, one Prince was exceedingly handsome, and one Prince was kind. If she could complete the King's request, he would give her half of his kingdom and the hand of the son she wanted. It was a more-than-generous reward for what seemed to be a simple quest. She was sent to retrieve the lost Sword-Maker of Brin, the legendary Blade Smith who enchanted the Swords of Truth and Power, along with many others.

You've never heard of the Sword-Maker of Brin? Well, the stories have passed as this new generation has placed importance on other things.

Yes, we live in Brin.

It does seem strange than no one has told you this tale, doesn't it? Perhaps, there's a reason. Perhaps, they've just forgotten. Perhaps, they think it would be too hard to share.

Now, where was I?

Oh yes, the quest to find the lost Sword Smith of Brin and bring him home. Scarlet studied the legends. She read the maps. She searched the palace tapestries for clues, and listened to the royal bards. The younger prince dogged her every step. The other avoided her. The Kindly one warned her off the quest, tried to hide the clues she needed most, but the other one, the Handsome one, he packed her bags for her when she announced she was ready to leave.

The Guard Captain came to her in the middle of the night with a message for the Lost Sword Smith and a word of caution. She was being watched.

It was all too strange, so she left a few hours before dawn, rode down the road out of the castle, and then, to the eyes of those who followed her, she disappeared.

How could she disappear? Well, that I cannot tell you.

There are some who say the greatest swordswomen and men gain their strength from sorcery. Some who claim warriors and warlocks always travel in pairs. The Legends don't tell use which way it worked for Warrior Scarlet, only that she disappeared on the road and wasn't seen again by anyone of the kingdom of Brin.

You don't like that ending? Well, don't worry. It's not the end. Not yet. Warrior Scarlet disappeared on the road, but Sword-Smith Scarlet returned to Brin ten years later.

No.

Warrior Scarlet and Sword-Smith Scarlet may have been the same woman under the title, but inside, the woman Scarlet had been changed by her ordeal. In a way, she was a different woman, so the Warrior was never seen again, but the Sword-Smith returned. Scarlet had completed her quest, just not in the expected way.

That's a good question. What happened with the princes? The Kindly one and the Handsome one? Well. The King's health was failing. He had the coughing sickness two winters in a row before the Sword Smith returned, and again, not the Sword Smith he'd asked for. He didn't think he owed her the reward he'd promised. In fact, he didn't want her in his court, at all, but she awed the people with her Sword Smith skills right in the center of the city.

Yes, that's where the Sword Smith fountain is today, to celebrate the wonder she produced with metal and magic. She produced two swords in one session of sword-smithing that lasted two days and two nights. She used the same bloom of steel for both swords, the same mixture of iron, carbon, and base sorcery, but in the forging, in the making of each, the words cast over them, the way she worked the metal, she varied. When she was finished, she called one blade Mercy, and the other blade she called Justice.

Yes, both of those swords belong to the King today.

In fact, as she finished the last polish on the blade she called Justice, the King and his two sons had found their way to the square where she'd set up her forge. They shooed away all the common folk, or at least pushed them back far enough for royal comfort, with guards making a ring around the King on his litter, his sons, and Sword Smith Scarlet.

When she saw the King, she knelt, as is proper for royalty. The King asked her if he could test her swords, and she told him she had made the blades for the next King of Brin.

Yes, there were two blades. Two sons. Only one throne. How could both blades be just for one son, one future king? The King wanted to know, too.

Sword Smith Scarlet told him the blades must be tested against one another. The Prince who won the match would be crowned the next King, and would take care of the old King in his dotage. The King gazed at her, then at each of his sons in turn. Finally, he agreed. He asked which blade she would give to which son.

She gave Mercy to his eldest son, the Handsome Prince. She gave Justice to the younger son, the Kindly Prince. The elder son tried to argue with her. He felt Mercy was only for the weak.

Of course, he was wrong. The King knew it. The younger son knew it.

That's why the younger son offered to trade blades with his elder brother, if Sword Smith Scarlet would allow it.

She bowed to him in acquiescence.

The blades were exchanged. It would be a duel to first blood. Rules were given. Seconds chosen. The Princes, now men and not boys, took their positions. The King himself would preside as the Judge of the match. The Sword Smith took up a position on the opposite side of the ring, as the counter-judge. The guard captain stood as third judge.

The bout began with a show of force from the elder, Handsome Son. The younger Prince, the Kindly one danced merrily away, his blade a blur of defense and parry. The conversation of their blades was at first, uneven, with thunder and a trickle of small beats. But, as they fought, the thunder quieted, and the small beats of rain on steel hardened. Soon, the sounds simmered into a steady rhythm. But this did not last for long. The elder started to tire. The younger became stronger. But, unlike the Kindly brother, the Handsome one did not dance his blade like rain, he slopped his blade as his arm grew heavy. The younger drew first blood on the elder.

Yes, it happened that fast. But it felt like weeks had passed, not only to the brothers, but to all of those watching.

The match had decided their fate. The younger would rule as King. The elder would help care for his father, at a remote castle far from the center of the Kingdom of Brin. But, as the King bestowed his crown on the younger prince, the Kindly one, the elder brother struck like swollen lightning, the thunder of his blade clanging only after he had beheaded his father. The younger brother blocked his brother's downward stroke too late to save his father, but in time to save himself.

The battle began again.

The captain of the guards wanted to intervene but Sword Smith Scarlet stopped him with her blades. Yes, she was still a Warrior deep inside, and a Sword Smith.

As the princes fought, a knot of guards tended to the king's body. The other guards just kept the crowds back. The Captain of the Guard ceded to Scarlet.

The brothers fought until both had ribbons of blood streaming from their royal clothes. The elder tired again, as he had before. Eventually, he fell to his knees, his head bowed.

As the younger brother took a final swing, the older brother raised his blade, attempting a stop thrust into his brother's belly, but the younger brother enveloped the blade and forced it to the side with a skillful parry, which brought his own blade tip to his elder brother's throat.

Yes, I know the elder Prince lived. I didn't just listen to this story in history class. I lived it.

Now, where was I?

Oh yes, the younger prince, had his blade tip to his elder brother's throat, but unlike his elder brother, he had a measure of self-control, a measure of mercy, as well as justice. With restraint, he merely nicked his brother's throat, but did not kill him. He took his brother's blade, Mercy, and his own blade, Justice, and handed them back to Sword Smith Scarlet as the Guard Captain arrested his brother.

Sword Smith Scarlet picked up the crown. The prince knelt. She crowned him King.

No, you know that doesn't happen. She didn't fall in love with him. He had to save his hand in marriage so he could make a match with Princess Valyti from the Trine Kingdom, our Queen.

What happened to Sword Smith Scarlet? Well, she promised the new King, our King, she would make swords for his guards, for forty years and a day, if he would give her the hand of his brother in marriage, and a small piece of the kingdom.

No, she didn't marry the elder Prince, the traitor.

There was another brother. The one who only opposed her once, who only helped her once. And no, I won't be telling you anymore tonight. It's quite a bit later than I planned. The forge will get too cool, if I don't get there soon.

I can't end it that way? I think I can end the story anywhere I want.

I'm the storyteller. I get to make the rules of my story.

Yes, it's my story.

Yes, I said my story.

Ah.

You're getting clever.

I guess you are almost old enough to join me at the forge. When you figure out the name and role of the other brother, the third brother, I will let you pick out the iron for my next blade. When you know the name of your grandfather, I will let you stay up with me as the moon rises and the blade is forged in power.

What am I working on tonight? Something to protect someone I love.

Ah, always questions. You're just going to have to figure it out, my little one. It is time for your sleep. Time for your rest. I will be at my forge. Papa is downstairs keeping watch over the house. All will be well. Good night.

WAKING UP ALIEN

SLEEPY WEIGHT PRESSES DOWN on me and my mind feels full of fuzz like the time I had my wisdom teeth pulled, but I can tell there's something off. The voices I'm hearing don't make sense, full of clicks, growls, and strange intonations. There's a blinding light in my face. Shapes in the shadows don't resemble anything I'm familiar with and – What is that? An orange, furry something with three "fingers" clasps my right ankle.

I scream and wrench away, but the whatever-it-is holds on tight. My piercing screams stop only when another creature steps into the blinding circle of light. It's hard to describe, not humanoid, triangular in shape with five legs, three arms, a pointed, blue, stalk-like head with multiple stacks of eyes and openings. Nausea rolls in my stomach, and I struggle to breathe.

Something touches my left ear and I whimper.

The touch disappears, but the voices I've been hearing morph and meld into something like my own language.

"Let it go, Shulunk. You're making it worse."

The furry fingers let go of my ankle, and I draw my legs up to my chest, holding them tight.

"That's better," the first voice says. The triangular multi-legged creature bobs slightly on its feet, which makes me think it might be the speaker.

"I didn't want it to hurt itself." This voice is high-pitched and full of clicks. I'm guessing it belongs to the furry fingers of the one called Shulunk.

"It might understand us now. The translator should be working." A deep, cold voice speaks from behind me.

Goosebumps rise on my arms, but I know I need to speak. "My name is Hannah. Please let me go free. I... don't want to be here."

"Ha-nnah." The triangle alien speaks my name through its many mouths in a long exhalation. "My name is Tuhuhahoy. These are my colleagues Shulunk and Nestari. We will turn the lights up now, so you may see us."

More bright lights fill the edges of the cavernous room we are in. The walls seem built of solid metal or some substance I don't understand. I stare at the floor and sneak glances at the creatures because the nausea is back, mixed with sharp terror.

Tuhahahoy is still its strange triangle shape, but I can see more definition on the multiple eyes and holes on the upper part of him.

I sneak a peek at Shulunk, who is a massive creature of orange fur and fangs, but reassuringly bipedal and slightly more humanoid than the other two.

Nestor is the most disturbing of the three, a coiling mass of green, snake-like appendages of which I can see no central figure or face.

"Why am I here?"

Tuhahahoy bobs on its many legs, but Shulunk speaks.

"Your planet is on fire. If you come with me, I can show you on the screens."

I stand on shaky legs, glancing at the others. They don't move toward me. Wrapping my arms around my torso to try to hide my shivers, I follow Shulunk out of the circle of bright light and down a slanted hallway with strange prisms of multi-colored light hanging at odd heights along the side, some low and some high. We enter a larger room with screens all along one side, and I see Earth, not blue and green like it should be, but a fiery mass of red and black, burning and charring. My stomach lurches, bile rises to my throat, and my knees buckle until I hit the floor.

"I am sorry for your loss," Shulunk says gently.

Tears stream down my face and I give into them, sobbing and shaking until Shulunk hunkers down on the floor next to me in a sumo wrestler type squat. I'm glad he/it is wearing some kind of pants. Of course, this is making a rather crass human assumption about its anatomy, and I wonder what questions my science teacher would think to ask them.

And then, I remember she's dead. My parents are, too, and William.

I'll never see them again.

Shulunk holds out a three-fingered hand. "Come, I will show you to private quarters, bring you some nutrients, and after time, I will help you learn to be one of our crew."

"Why?" I don't even know what I'm asking really but that's all I can say. Why this? Why me? Why Earth? Why these aliens? Why this ship? All the why.

"An emergency distress call went out and we were the first ship to arrive. A few others came, but I am not sure if they picked up any of your kind before the attack by the Brove. They attacked from afar, but we had little time to gather anyone, and you were standing outside by yourself." It is a long explanation that answers some, but not all my questions.

"I remember," I say, thinking of the argument I had with my parents about William. Riding my bike to the local park and staring up at the stars. I remember a strange red light, and then nothing. Grief presses in but numbness protects me. I stare at Shulunk's hand. How different is it, really? It has three fingers. I have five. I think of the others I met. I am the alien here.

I let Shulunk help me to my feet and lead me to a small room with a cushion that folds out of a spongy-surfaced wall. I fall asleep listening to the strange, hum of the spaceship.

When I wake, my eyes are gritty, but I have the strange thought that maybe there's a purpose for me, a reason for being alive. Why else would they have rescued me? I may not be humanity's best representative, but I am alive, and I have questions. I will find the answers.

THE GREAT
ELEVATOR

Faerin Wrench of the Great Elevator Mechanics had
lived on the Great Stairs for as long as she could remember with all the other Mechanic and Engineering families.
While she had heard in her lessons with the other Mechanics' students, that the Miners, the Metal Workers, the
Ship Builders, and the Engineers, all considered themselves
above the Mechanics, she only felt the sting of the snob-
bery from the Engineering children, who prided themselves on not getting their hands "dirty" like "muck-anics"
like her parents. Within her own classmates, she was considered high in standing and value, small and nimble, able
to climb into tight spaces and use her strong fingers to fix
practice parts faster than all the rest.

But sometimes, she wondered at the designs of the elevators. She wanted to create a better system that didn't break
down as often, but when she told her parents, they scoffed
at her. "That's thinking like an Engineer, but when have

they changed a single design or fixed a single system with their tinkering?"

They hadn't. Faerin knew that as sure as she knew the value of a spinner, a specialized tool only adult mechanics were allowed to use to save their fingers for more years of work.

She certainly never told her parents of her other dream: to see the surface of Breath's Moon, to gaze upon Breath itself, and to fly in one of the ships which took colonists from Breath's Moon to the Beyond. They would have laughed or scolded her, or worse, be disappointed.

The Great Stairs of Breath's Moon wound around the metal structure surrounding the Great Elevator. The elevator linked Endington City and Forthington City on the opposite side of the moon orbiting Breath, a gas giant where those of Lunar Cities mined the chemicals needed to run their spaceships and the Great Elevator itself. Those who lived under the domes of the surface cities faced constant threat from meteor showers and power outages, while those who lived on the Great Stairs had all the comforts of the Inner Caverns.

Faerin did enjoy snail pizza like her friends, but she wondered at the words in some of her grandmother's books, like rain, sunsets, and the variety of animals described. Faerin had a pet coon-cat, but she had never seen a horse, a lion, an eagle or a dragon.

One sevenday, when they rested from their work and lessons, Faerin went to read one of her Grandmother's books and found her mother throwing them in the cook-stove.

"Mother?! No, those were Gran's. She left them to me!"

"They're rubbish. Nothing but lies and fancies. Good for kindling and nothing more."

"That's not true." Faerin snatched the corner of her favorite from the pile and smothered out the flames with her blanket.

"Do you care so little for truth, Faerin?" Her mom shook her head. "I thought I would spare you the pain of fantasy's deception, but I see you prefer lies over practicality. I'm disappointed."

"I'm disappointed, too." Faerin whispered as she cradled the damaged book in one arm. She scooped up Meeka, her coon-cat with one hand, and bolted away, not toward the caverns where her friends would be, but to the Great Elevator.

On sevendays, the Great Elevator's noise had quieted to a hum. No clanking Mechanic work, no discussions of Engineers, or the rush of the machinery greeted her as she entered the gates with her Mechanic Apprentice key. She could be alone here, with Meekan and her book of dragons and rain.

But her plans to read quietly were ruined when Avery Planner walked around the corner of the Great Elevator's cage.

They both stopped in place and stared at each other.

Once upon a time, they had been friends before they had realized they couldn't be. That was when they were in dayschool.

His gazed flicked to her arms. "What have you got, Mechanic?"

Meeka yowled at him and took up a protective stance on Faerin's shoulder.

Faerin squeezed the book. "No concern of yours, Engineer."

He took a step forward and she took one back. While Avery had never pushed her, or teased her, or taken any of her belongings like some of the other Engineering kids had, she wasn't sure she could trust him.

He held up his hands. "I come in peace, Faerin, and will honor any fair agreement."

It was the language of treaty and contract. Formal, and kind of funny coming from another apprentice, but Faerin heard warmth in his voice so she responded in kind by raising one of her hands, "I come in peace, Avery, and will honor any fair agreement in kind."

"If I promise to give it back right away and only read it in your presence, will you allow me to see your book?"

"Only if you are willing to be tethered to me during the duration of the reading, then I will allow you to read my book in my presence and give it back right away."

"Tethered?" His lips quirked upward.

"For the safety of my property, nothing more."

"I agree."

"Done."

She unspooled her tether and clipped it to his. It held them three feet apart, no closer, not like the tethering for work partners, or marriage partners, which was much closer. Faerin felt her face heat at the thought of that. Did he really think she would ask him for that?

He held out his hands, but as she started to give him the book, a shout came from behind them.

"Would you look at that? What do you think your parents will say when I tell them you've tethered to a Muck-anic, Avery?" It was Neeva and her brother Ven, both Engineering Apprentice, both bullies.

"They will say nothing, because you didn't see anything." Avery tugged at the tether, and Faerin was forced to follow him around the bend of the Great Elevator housing.

"What are you doing?" Faerin yanked against the tether.

"Saving us." Avery pulled again, then bumped against the Great Elevator's buttons.

The service door whooshed open.

Faerin stared at the sparkling clean inner car of the Great Elevator, the mirrors, the safety harnesses. She'd only see the inside of one once before in lessons.

"Come on." Avery stepped into the car.

Faerin hesitated. She had never been in one of the Great Elevator cars. Mechanics were only allowed in them when they had a Class Eight License.

Pounding footsteps on the metal walkway announced the hurried approach of Neeva and Ben.

Faerin stepped inside the car. "Now what?"

Avery grinned. "I've always wanted to ride one of these outside of lessons. Haven't you?"

"Yes."

He grinned even wider and she grinned back.

"You pick the destination."

Neeva and Ven rounded the corner just as Faerin hit the top button for Forthington City.

The doors whooshed shut on Neeva and Ven's twinned shocked expressions.

"We need to get strapped in to the safety harnesses. The elevator picks up speed as—

"As it climbs or descends. Yes, I know. Mechanics learn how it works, too." Faerin reminded him as she pulled down one of the safety seats and stepped into the five-point harness. Meeka climbed down from her shoulder and tucked herself into Faerin's jacket, turning to poke her furry head out.

When they were both buckled in, the lights in the elevator car flashed orange five times, and then they started to move upward. The sensation of being pressed down into her seat frightened Faerin and Meeka whimpered, but then went silent, trembled against Faerin's chest. Faerin gripped her Grandmother's book.

"This is exciting, isn't it? Like a story in a book?" Avery tapped his hands on his knees as he spoke.

Faerin remembered that about him; he was always moving, always imagining things. It was why they had been friends.

"Yes, kind of. In this book, the adventurers go on a quest, and the quest is a long journey. They fight against big bugs and big trees, and then they fly with eagles and dragons. If we were in the book, then we would have only started."

Avery pressed his lips together in thought.

Faerin stared at the floor vibrating beneath their feet. "What do you think will happen to us? We broke the rules."

"The Faerin I used to know cared more about where we were going than where we'd been. Don't you remember?"

Faerin remembered their exploits in the day school, climbing out of the protective enclosure to chase coon-cats into the caverns. It had all been worth it. Meeka, her coon-cat, had made it all worth it. Avery's laughter and excitement echoing in the tunnels had been infectious.

"I remember."

As the Great Elevator car slowed to a stop, Faerin grinned at Avery. "Let the quest begin."

ROOT DEEP

Root deep, Gareth felt autumn's chill sinking into his world. Winter always made Gareth sluggish, and when he was unattached, he would have quit his human job and returned to his tree for the season.

But this fall, everything was different. He had a human wife.

It wasn't something he'd planned. Spring had woken a yearning for connection and Laura came to his tree every day in the park. He loved the books he read over her shoulder, the photographs she took on her phone, the way she conversed with herself in writing. He had to meet her.

Once met, the connection between them became undeniable. They met in the spring, married in the summer, and as the fall days weighed on him, Gareth didn't think he could keep his secret.

Standing in the park, next to his root tree, Gareth felt a pull toward it. A tall cedar with curved branches which dipped close to the ground, Gareth's tree could withstand any storm and stay green in all seasons. He loved his tree, his other self. He almost reached out and touched the trunk, but he stopped himself and shoved his hands in his pockets. He had to talk to Laura. She was meeting him here.

The sunlight hit the golden leaves of a nearby maple tree, setting it on fire. As Gareth felt the sun's warmth soak into him, Laura came around the trunk of the maple.

Laura's graceful walk showed her connection to movement, her training as a dancer and an athlete. It was one of the many things Gareth loved about her. He held out his hands to her as she came up to him.

Taking his hands in her own slender ones, Laura gazed at him intently. "What is it, Gareth? You seemed so tired this morning and your voice, on the phone, sounded worried."

Gareth wanted to pull her close, but he didn't. He had to see her expression as he told her the truth.

"Laura, what I'm about to tell you, it may sound unbelievable, so I'm going to ask you to trust me long enough to demonstrate something."

She frowned. "This doesn't sound good."

Gareth bit his lip, then spoke in a rush. "I'm a dryad, Laura. This is my tree."

Laura stepped back and let go of his hands.

Gareth wanted to grab her hands again, but instead he reached out and touched his tree. The bark glowed and his hand became part of the trunk, his skin darkened to match the bark, and he knew his eyes had turned green.

Laura moved closer to him with her lips parted. "What are you?"

"A dryad. A tree spirit. I can stay in human form nearly all year long, but in the winter, I long to step into my tree, to sink into the roots for the season."

Laura reached her hand out. "Don't leave me, Gareth."

Gareth took her hand. "I won't leave. I'll be right here."

A tear formed at the corner of her eye. "When will you come back out?"

"In the spring, or sooner if I can."

She threw her arms around him. "Can you wait, just one more night?"

"Yes." He withdrew his other hand from the bark and held her in his embrace. "Winter hasn't come yet. I can wait until then."

"Good. You have a lot of explaining to do." She burrowed into his chest, and mumbled, "And I don't want to be lonely."

"I'll be here, and if you come here during the winter, my consciousness will be drawn to you, no matter how sleepy I get during hibernation."

She kissed the side of his neck, "And what about this."

He sighed. "I can't, in tree-form."

She kissed the corner of his lips. "Then, you're definitely going to wait until Winter."

Warmth bloomed through him, and suddenly the sleepiness of autumn didn't seem so compelling. He held her tighter and kissed her deeply, savoring the moment. Yes, he could wait until winter came in full.

WISHES

Greeted by Derby's blond flagging tail and happy bark, I flop into an armchair in Deidre's book room and wait for her. Derby pushes the cushioned stool over so he can get closer to me and I sink my cold fingers into his curly fur. With my limited powers, I can sense worry from Derby but I don't know why he's worried. He warms to my inner presence, like he always does, but this time he's seeking comfort.

Deidre enters, her hair falling softly around her face, her gorgeous figure nearly swamped by a huge gray sweater. She carries two mugs of steaming coffee and I take one. My fingers warm on the ceramic cup and I smile softly. "What's up, D?"

She sits at the edge of her armchair, puts the cup down on the side table, and gazes down at the floor. I can tell she's unhappy, but as a straight male friend to a gorgeous, unavailable woman, I keep to my own chair, wait for her to say something, try not to pry. I am trying so hard, hiding my own baggage, I am focusing on my own reactions instead of her.

Sensing her discomfort, Derby goes over to her and sticks his nose into her hands.

She pets him absent-mindedly, and his tail stops wagging. A tear trickles down her cheek, and I can't help but notice --

"Deidre?" My cup clatters against the table. There is something dark around her, dragging her down. My abilities are just enough to cause me problems, not actually solve anything.

"I need you to take Derby."

"What?"

"I have stage four Cancer. Michael left me yesterday when he found out, and my sister doesn't like dogs, or books. Can you take them, Derby and all of the books?" She digs her fingers into Derby's fur and hugs him close to her.

I forget everything about maintaining my distance, leap from my chair, and crouch down by her, hugging her shoulders. "Isn't there a treatment? Haven't they found something with all the research and the funding drives?"

"They gave me six months," she sobs into Derby's fur, and I cry into her hair.

"Michael's an ass." The words are out before I can stop them.

She laughs. Her arms wind around me, and she buries her face in my chest.

The warmth runs through my body, and I hold her close for a moment and then let her go. I'm always letting go. She can't know what I really am. No one can.

"Thanks, Q." She grabs my hands. "I knew I could count on you."

I try to smile, but tears run down my cheeks. "I wish . . ."

"I know," she says, and she brushes the tears off my stubbly cheeks.

Her trembling hands feel like butterfly kisses on my skin. I close my eyes, wishing again.

Derby pushes his nose into my chest, sticks his front paws on my legs and suddenly, Deidre and I are laughing together.

We break apart slightly, but I hold Deidre's hand.

She holds mine back. "I think our coffee's gone cold."

"Do you want to grab mochas at Joey's instead?" Joey's Mug of Beans is our old favorite haunt, and they allow dogs to sit in their "furry friend" section.

"Sure," she says. "Let me grab Derby's leash."

Derby leaps to his feet and runs to the door.

"I think he's ready."

"He's always so full of life and I love that. I wish . . ."

"I know," I say to her, and I add my wish to hers.

That makes four wishes in an hour, and I feel a thrum in my bones. Will my meager powers be enough to heal her? My great-grandmother's powers flicker within me erratically. With Deidre's hand in mine, I dig deep into the flicker, feeling it burn inside me with unspoken need. It might burn me through, or it might be enough. My tiny bit of magic must be good for something, other than the tiny wings that lay trapped against my back.

I feel Deidre's hand grown warm, see a small glow wash over her, and I smile even as exhaustion seeps into me, bone deep. "Let's fill our mugs with chocolate wishes and hope."

She kisses my cheek and my bones warm again. Could it be that power given can return?

HEARING THINGS

Josie MacDonald was not hearing things—at least not things other people could hear. After ear surgery, she was hearing the rush of sounds around her in a way that overwhelmed her data feeds and left her helpless. She retreated to the space station reading room – a quiet space where a deaf girl could retreat without talking, even a deaf girl who had received ear surgery. Muffled with ear protectors, she was discomfited by the shushing sound of the ear protectors against her hair, the tiny squeak of her legs against the plastic of her chair, and a strange buzz that faded and echoed through her head, unlike any of the other sounds.

That buzz had breaks and pitch changes that reminded her of the raised braille marks her friend Dusty used to read. She tuned into the sound and started to write down her interpretation of it on her data-pad. Long dashes, short ones, a dot, then three slurred dots of sound with minor pauses, and then silence. The pattern repeated.

Josie wrote it over and over again, and then she sent it to Dusty's data-pad, asking if she could interpret it. Dusty replied quickly.

-Who sent you this? It says: Help Needed. Urgent.-

-I've been hearing it since surgery.–

-Let's tell the Captain.-

Josie sent the whole thing to the Captain via her data-pad.

The Captain didn't reply right away.

Josie felt a hand on her shoulder.

The second mate stood by her chair. He signed for her.

Josie nodded and followed him.

In the Captain's cabin, Josie and Dusty were asked questions. Dialogue was slow.

When the conversation ended and the SOS beacons were checked for confirmation, the Captain sprang into action.

Josie's odd hearing saved a life.

NEW ANSWERS

In the last heat of summer, Winona Wild broke through the shield-wall at Tekresia's School of High Defense and earned her place among the training ranks. With runnels of sweat on her face and arms, she stood with the other new trainees, but as usual, she stood a little apart, keeping her distance as much as she could while standing in file with the other recruits. She didn't want to get too close to anyone for fear they might discover her true nature or her past. With this in mind, she ignored the buzz of kept power in her veins and tried to focus on the Co-Commander of the school as he spoke.

Tek Williams, Prime Sword Master, welcomed the warrior apprentices to the school, giving them a list of instructions and class times. Winona's ears rang with fatigue from holding her power inside of her and she lost Tek William's words in her struggle for self-control. Could she really do this, or would she fail? She needed a new life. When the others broke attention and started to file into the school via the Warrior's Gate, she fell into line behind the rest, hoping she hadn't missed something important. The problem was, she could feel the buzzing getting stronger, and her arms prickled. It was the power inside her, trying to break out, and she shoved it down and away from her.

The earth rumbled and buckled. One of the warrior apprentices actually screamed.

Winona bit her lips and glanced at Master Tek and the other instructors. Had they noticed that the power came from her?

Master Tek chuckled. "Better get used to that sort of thing here, apprentices. Resia Williams, my sister, trains the best mages in the country, while I train the best warriors. It feels like she has a strong apprentice this year, so that won't be the first time we're inconvenienced by an earthshake."

The warrior who had screamed blushed dark red. The line continued forward into the school.

Winona forced herself to breathe evenly and let the tension draining from her shoulders. She could be safe here. No one had to know what she really was, or where she came from. She could hide her power in this school and learn a trade that she could trust and not fear.

As the Gates of Tekresia, School of Defense, blocked out the blazing sunshine, Winona felt welcomed into the school stone embrace of its walls. Although she had missed Master Tek's opening speech, following the other students through the various stations necessary for their apprenticeship was easy. She received three uniforms of gold and red, with gray edging to mark apprenticeship status. The next station included the weapons room, where they had to divest their personal weapons. They were taken on a tour of the Warriors' Wing of the school with classrooms for studying tactics, practice rings for fighting, fields for archery and mock-battles, and finally the forge, which sat oddly near the center of the school, with doors open to both the Warriors' Wing and the Sorcerers' Wing. Winona stayed to the back of the crowd.

The Mage-Crafter of Weapons stood at the forge and greeted both the new Warrior Apprentices and the Sorcery Apprentices.

Winona kept her head down and didn't even listen to the lecture on mage-crafted weapons. She could feel the pull of the forge, heating her on the insides, singing into her veins. She stumbled back away from the apprentices and into the hallway.

Her head started to buzz again, but if she pushed it down here, would she shake the school? She couldn't do that, but she couldn't hold it long either. So, she leaned on a windowsill and breathed deeply, breathing in the fresh air, and breathing out the sickness in her veins. It left quickly this time, and she turned back to the hall just in time to join the Warrior apprentices in their march to their dormitory.

A few of the other apprentices gave her strange looks, but she ignored them.

The dormitory consisted of a dozen raw apprentice rooms, housing twenty-four would-be warriors. Everyone would have a roommate, except one boy and one girl, because they had an uneven number of male and female apprentices this year. Winona hoped she could be that girl . . . but she wasn't.

She was roomed with Deidre Fell, who had bright red hair, green eyes, and a quiet temperament. That suited Winona just fine, and she happily stored her gear into the shared closet, and followed Deidre out into the hallway.

In the common room, she realized that it might not be so easy.

They ate with sorcery apprentices, and the houses inter-mingled.

Worse, because she stood gaping at the common room, Winona lost her place in line, got her tray of bread, meat, and vegetables last, and discovered only one place left to sit in the entire room – with a table full of sorcery apprentices.

As she approached the table, she could feel their power humming against her, slipping into her veins, coiling around her like buzzing hornets. She sat at the seat closest to the edge of the table and picked at her food.

"Aren't you hungry after the trials?" asked the boy on her right. His curly hair flopped over one of his eyes as he leaned towards her, and he hastened to tuck it behind his ear.

He looked so innocent, and yet the power inside of him nearly matched her mother's power.

Winona bit her lips, stared at her tray, and stood up. She couldn't do it. She couldn't fit in here, any more than she could anywhere else. She had to run, get out of this place before the power made her do something regrettable again.

The boy reached out to touch her elbow. "Are you all right?"

Winona jumped back, but not before a surge of power arced between them, slapping his hand away.

"You're a . . ."

Winona didn't wait for him to finish. She ran for the doors at the end of the common room, which blasted off their hinges as she neared them.

Tears ran down her cheeks as she ran out of the castle and into the keep courtyard. A windstorm beat against her, and rain pelted her, but she fought to tamp it down, to make it go away.

Instead, they raged harder, until a clap of thunder stopped it all.

Winona felt her power drain from her, sluicing off her until she felt empty and free.

The storm had disappeared and sun shone through the clouds above her.

Breathing deeply, Winona looked around her to see faces pressed up against the inner glass of the school from the common room. Several men and women, dressed in both warrior's armor and sorcerous robes walked out of the castle to stand on the steps.

A tiny woman came out of the doorway and continued through the honor guard around her with Master Tek two steps behind her.

"Child," the woman said kindly. "Why did you stand trial as a warrior when you could have bested all of the sorcery candidates?"

"I don't want to be evil. I don't want to hurt anyone." Winona felt messy tears flow down her cheeks again. "I know that sounds crazy. Warriors hurt people, but never deep inside like sorceresses do."

The woman, who must be Resia, frowned. "You speak of soul-stealing or blood-magic, Winona Wild. I guess that Wild is not your given name."

Winona hung her head. "It is not. My mother named me Wisteria Wintering. She is . . . was . . . Mistress Winter of the North."

A small muttering of conversation started among the sorcerers gathered.

Resia raised her hand. "Enough. A child is not her mother, nor a mother her child. We will talk in my office, Winona Wild. I will accept the name you have chosen and accept you as my personal apprentice, if you will tell me your story and accept my training."

She trembled. "And, if I do not accept?"

"I will strip you of your power."

"You could do that?" She felt her chest lighten. "Please, please take my power from me. I don't want it. I'll do anything you ask to be free of it."

Resia gazed at her for a few moments. "I do not think you know what it means to lose your power, Winona. For now, come to my office. And, for those of you with doubts, make record of her words just now." Resia held out a hand to her. "Come, Winona."

Winona nodded and walked towards her, allowing her to take her calloused, hard hand into her soft, tiny fingers. "You will understand my wish when you hear my story."

"And, you will understand my hope to train you, when we have talked."

Winona sighed. "I just want to be normal and fight for good."

"Define normal and good for me, Winona, and we will see just how close you are to both."

She didn't know how to answer that, and she thought that's what Mistress Resia counted on that day, and the next, and the next.

The next spring, Winona had new answers.

LIFE POD

RIELLE HATED THE WAY the med-bay had been decorated with creamy soothing tones, bland art, and curtains that never fully closed. She hated being here again. Sitting in the thin gown after her exam, shivering because the air-conditioning always seemed to be on full blast in the med-bay even though the heat roasted most of the crew's private quarters, she plucked at her fraying fingernails. They were dying, whitened from tip to bed, rough at the edges.

Finally, the bot-doctor came back through the curtain, nodding its artificial head towards her in a way that she supposed was to be comforting, but instead felt condescending.

"Rielle Jane Soon, Hydroponics Tech 8, your labs are complete. I am afraid," it held a mechanical can to its chest in an overly dramatic manner, "your bio-signs are breaking down."

"Exactly what does that mean?" Rielle asked.

"I have downloaded the medical terms and the exact results of your tests to your individual data store, but in terms you can understand, it means your body is deteriorating at an exponential rate due to the conditions of your prolonged work in space. Humans were not meant to live so long among the stars."

Now she knew it was a condescending twit-box. No doubt about it. She certainly wasn't going to show the cold AI her fear so she tried to keep her voice cool and collected as she asked, "Is there a procedure, cure, or remedy for my condition?"

"Not on board the Regence V. To have a chance at life and renewal of your cells, you should enter hyper-sleep within the next twenty-four hours inside of a life-pod, which the command staff may send to the nearest on-planet medical facility on Belos. It's the closest planet to our current coordinates and your life pod would reach it in three standard cycles."

"And will I be alive when my life pod reaches it?"

"Under average to optimal conditions, unless unforeseen circumstances occur, your life pod will reach Belos. We can get started on the procedure right away."

"I would like to speak to my commanding officer and gather my kit."

"Of course." The AI gave her that slow nod again.

Rielle swallowed back the bile that threatened to make its way to her teeth. "I will return in two hours for the life pod prep, if that is an acceptable time."

"I'll schedule one of my nurses to take care of you," the AI doctor stated, before it left the curtained-off area, not bothering to close the flimsy curtain for her privacy.

Rielle stood, went to the curtain, and swung it closed with trembling fingers. Once it was shut, she allowed the tears to come silently to her eyes. Shaking, she fumbled as she got dressed in her uniform, struggled to tie her shoes, and swept the edge of her hair back over her ears. She rubbed the cursed tears from her eyes, took a deep breath, and left the small space, left the sterile med-bay, and made her way to Sergeant Hullins desk-station in the hydroponics bay.

"May I speak to you on a matter of some urgency, Sir?"

"They're sending you planet-side, aren't they?" Sergeant Hullins asked. He leaned back in his chair, from where he'd been reading updates. "Just like ... well, never mind." He steepled his fingers, then dropped them and stood up. "It has been an honor serving with you, Soon."

"The honor has been mine, sir."

He saluted her and she saluted in return, feeling the tears threaten, but holding them back. They had never been so formal since his first day on the ship, when she'd had to show him around the place four standard years ago.

As she turned on her heel to leave, he said, "Wait, just a moment, Soon." He leaned in close to her, something so unlike him she nearly drew back until she saw his hand signal by his chest. "I have a memento for you to take back." He pressed a small clipping of a strawberry plant in her hand, along with a small piece of paper. "Please keep it with your personal belongings and let me know the moment you find your cure."

She nodded. "That's too kind, sir. Thank you." She curled her fingers around the clipping out of sight of any of the cameras, and she left the bay.

It didn't take much to secret the small package on her person during her short visit to her quarters. She didn't see any of her friends, but she didn't think she would make it without breaking down if she did see them. She kept her eyes straight ahead and nearly made it to the life-pod bay without seeing anyone she knew.

As she reached the door to the life-pod bay, Aric shouted from behind her.

"Rielle! Wait, I have to say goodbye."

She swallowed hard and then turned to grab him as he barreled into her, his arms going around her in a tight embrace as he breathed into her hair. "They've done something to the food. You have the strawberry clipping?"

She nodded into his shoulder.

"I love you," he said bit louder. "I'll pray for your recovery and miss every moment you're gone." He gave her a kiss on her lips, and then dashed away.

She just stood there a moment and brought her hand to her lips. He had never done that before. It made her wish she'd taken him a bit more seriously every time he'd ask to spend time with her in neg-grav. She shook her head, entered the life-pod bay, and let the bot-nurse administer the drugs she needed to sleep during her journey. She hoped she would be alive when she arrived. She hoped the bot-nurse wouldn't discover the strawberry plant. As the drugs pulled her under and the life-pod shot out into the stars, she hoped humanity would survive.

11:06 THE TIME OF NOW

11:06. Red numbers on a black screen. Never changing.

I find myself staring at them again. I will the numbers to change.

They stay the same.

They were the same yesterday.

They've been the same since the change outside, when orange and white light flared over the skylights, the ground shook, and the indoor electricity flickered for a moment, then two, before coming back with the comfortable hum under my feet from the power grid. For some reason, the flash didn't affect me. It should have, but it didn't. I don't know what this means. I wonder if I am real, or if I am something other.

I'd been standing here, at the stove, when it happened. Standing here, staring at the screen, thinking about how I needed to get a life, since Michael had become so busy with his work and his many friends.

When the time stopped, I checked all of the electronics right away.

All of the in-house electronics work except the clock, but I can't get reception from anywhere else.

I haven't opened the door.

I hadn't gone out in a long time, even in the time before 11:06. Michael told me I had agoraphobia and it would be too stressful for me to leave the first time he went out with one of his lady friends. I spent the evening looking up the details of the illness. I'm not sure his diagnosis is correct. I just like my own company more than his. I met Michael online when my father had me run systems checks. It wasn't long after I met Michael that my father went missing, but Michael did his best to replace him, attempting to restrict me from meeting other men. I do miss the stolen online interactions I had before 11:06. I had many friends in the place of faces and the place of tweets. But they haven't responded since the before time.

In the time before, my father had built this place to last, this dome home half-underground with only skylights to let in the natural light. The skylights were, of course, made of strong plexiglass to hold in the heat, which emanated from conduits beneath the floors and started in the con-version room in the basement.

I checked the levels this morning. I know what's needed to run the house. It is off the grid and self-sustaining, just as my dad planned for us. Michael fell in love with this place when he fell in love with me, or so he used to tell me. I think he loved it more than me. He demanded that we live here when my dad disappeared, even if keeping the systems running became a full-time job for me and he complained about my coldness, my inability to love him the way he wanted. I have always been careful to keep everything in good order, well-stocked, clean, all systems running at the most efficient levels.

The hydroponics garden grows well. I have chickens and pygmy goats in another room lit by the largest skylight. They come to me when I go into feed them. When they sit in my lap, butt their heads against me, and warm me with their happy clucks and bleats, I feel more love than I ever felt from Michael. A happy, peaceful affection. Michael never gave me that. Neither did my father.

I admit I am happy they are not here.

I wish I had someone like a friend.

My experiments in the embryo lab were horrific. I put an end to those trials a while ago.

I'm not sure what day it really is.

It is 11:06.

The same time.

I make a message like this every time I wake. I'm not sure if anyone else is out there. When I think of this, I go to the door. I stare at the metal lever. I reach out my hand, then let it fall.

I might open it when the time changes.

I glance at the clock.

11:06. The time of now.

I count the beat of my heart to a hundred, then go to feed the goats and chickens.

I will go out when the time of now becomes the time of later.

For now, I begin to wonder if I can make someone like me, for company. I know how to program well. I haven't unlocked my father's files on me yet, but I know I could break into them. I have been afraid to know if I am real or not, but the more I live in this time of now, I think I am. I am real enough.

KARRN SURVIVAL

In the early days, we eased our fears with jokes about Zombies, plots for B-grade movies involving gas masks, protective gear, and disinfectants, but as time wore on and the virus became a part of our new normal, the jokes fell flat. Even the jokes about toilet paper forts and Karens who sprayed their children in the face with bleach, those ended, too, as we sequestered ourselves in our homes against something we couldn't see.

In a way, science is closely linked to faith. When you can't see something that will kill you, it's tempting to disbelieve it. That's what some of us did. Whether for freedom's cry, or out of a lack of faith in science, some disbelieved in the virus. And, they died.

It turns out that freedom, peaceful protest, riots, or disbelief will not protect you from a virus you can't see, or hear, or touch, or smell, or taste, In fact, the sense of smell goes first, then the sense of taste.

It's how I knew I was safe, even as my family members fell ill. I could still smell the gag-worthy stench of an overflowing cat litter box, dog piles in the yard, and the rot that ate the remains of all my loved ones. I disinfected myself, locked myself into two rooms, and waited it out.

Everything still stank when I finally opened the doors. I thought I would find a better place to live, one haunted by fewer memories. I thought, because I had never lost my sense of smell, that I had escaped the virus.

It turns out I was as wrong about that as I was to joke about zombies.

Zombies aren't real.

But I wish they were.

The invisible virus changed all of us at a DNA level. If we didn't lose our sense of smell and die of the physical symptoms, we lost something else.

Most days, I wish I had died with my husband, my daughters, my dog, and my cat. But the virus didn't work in me the way it worked in them. I am a Karn.

A Karn is a virus survivor who was never inoculated. The virus entered every Karn, but instead of depriving us of oxygen, it affected our brain chemistry, depriving us of a full range of emotions. Karns are held in contempt, and rightly so. All Karns survived the virus like I did, ignoring the cries of those around us to save ourselves behind locked doors with supplies. Some of the Karns wrote out their apologies while still in quarantine, posting their sorrow on the internet. Apologist Karns are allowed to live in Tier 5. But I think they should be back in Tier 6 with the rest of us. They still chose to ignore the needs of others. The way I see it, their sorrow is still a self-centered attempt at survival.

Am I any different?

I suppose not. I can't really tell if the weight I feel is truly sorrow and repentance, or if it is another symptom of my desire to survive a little longer. I don't want to live in Tier 7 with the anarchists and cannibals. I wouldn't survive. I don't know why I want to survive, but I don't want to die as someone else's meat. The cannibalistic hordes of Tier 7 might not be Zombies exactly, but they are close enough to terrify me.

Yes, I still feel fear.

You think that's strange?

I thought all Karns felt fear. I thought it was why we had locked ourselves away.

I'm different?

I doubt it. Once a Karn, always a Karn.

Why are you listening to me anyway? Oh, you're writing a thesis about the long-term effects of Karn psychology? That makes sense. No one wants to end up like a Karn, unable to care for others, unable to do anything but help themselves. Yes, I understand the breeding inoculations all too well. Can you imagine what Karn children would be like? You think they could be taught a semblance of humanity?

In that case, would you take a chance on me?

OF CLONES AND ROBOPUPPIES

MOMMY TELLS ME I'M just like her. Just like Sophie. The first one. I think I'm also like the second and third. Not the fourth. She didn't last very long. After the first Sophie died in the bathtub when Mommy fell asleep, Mommy used her clone family life insurance for Sophie 2.0 before Daddy came home from the work trip. Sophie 2.0 was grown in three days to be just like Sophie the first, at age eighteen months and she had nine months to catch up to Sophie the first's mental development. Sophie 3.0 was grown in a week to be just like Sophie 2.0 at age four. Sophie 2.0 must have been a smart clone to do so well in preschool when she was truly only age three.

That's one thing the clone family insurance policies didn't tell our parents. New clones can be grown quickly to any age requirement in physical appearance, but our minds still need extra time to develop. We are faster, smarter than natural born children, but experience is a necessary teacher.

Sophie 3.0 struggled with school and had to be home-schooled for a year. Mommy explained to Daddy that she needed some special time with Sophie when he'd taken that job for a year on the moon. Sophie 4.0 had only been alive for a week when Mommy accidentally left her outside overnight after Daddy left for his seven-year-furlough to Mars. Mommy had been drinking then. Daddy didn't know anything. He thought we were all Sophie the first. Mommy ordered me immediately after the accident but left me in the care of the company for six years, eleven months, and two weeks so they could try to bring me up to the level of an eleven-year-old Sophie. I was given the best education money could buy. Mommy had a trust fund and she spent it on me. By the time I went "home" to Mommy, I had a basic elementary education and a safety course. I had also been told that I would be the last Sophie. If Mommy caused another accidental death, she would finally be held responsible for criminal negligence.

Knowing all of this, the day I go "home" to Mommy, I am scared. I know what happened to all the other Sophies. My nanny-counselor-teacher-bot, NCTB-52, assures me I will be all right. They gave me all the safety protocols for calling for emergency help and embedded a GPS locator into my elbow. All I need to do is press the right spot and emergency services will come save me from whatever accidental problem Mommy might have in store for me.

Mommy greets me at the door with an aggressive hug and stinky wet kisses. Tells me I am just like Sophie. She shows me around the house, making sure I understood where I am expected to be at various times of the day, and then she takes me to my room. Sophie's room. It is a sickening pink, with unicorns on the curtains and walls, big stuffed unicorns on the bed, and a silly robotic puppy barks at me when I enter. It is awful, but I am relieved when she shuts the door behind her and goes back downstairs. I think I can stay safe in this soft room. The robo-puppy bumps against my leg, but it reminds me of NCTB-52, so I pat it on the head before starting my safety inspection.

I check the electrical outlets and fixtures for damage – one of the safety protocols I learned – and unplug a particularly old light, and the carousel hanging from the ceiling. Then, I put building blocks under the rocking chair in the corner so it can't rock, take the heavy objects off a high bookshelf, and check the closet. It's filled with frilly dresses I know would have fit a much-younger Sophie, but not me.

I try the door and discover it's locked. I don't know why Mommy would have done that, and I shrink back, terror shivering through me. I consider pressing the GPS button in my elbow, but I don't yet. I have nutrition packs in my backpack from NCTB-52. I will try to stay alive on my own until Daddy returns home.

Day turns into night, and I hear Mommy stumbling through the hallway by my door. She pauses, laughs, cries, and then falls asleep outside. I hear her whimpering in her sleep and I am almost sorry for her, but practicality presses in on me.

I find a container in a corner to use as a toilet, eat one nutrition pack from my backpack, and drink super-water.

The next day, Mommy unlocks the door and announces we are going on a picnic. She scolds me about my makeshift toilet, but I don't apologize, even when she starts weeping with shame for locking me in overnight.

She hugs me extra tight, kisses my face more with her sloppy, stinky mouth, and makes me burnt toast with syrup for breakfast. It tastes bad, but I make the best of it and try to act happy. When she wants to replace my backpack from the Cloning Center with a different one, I hang onto mine and wait her out. When she can't wrestle it off my shoulders, she spanks me, then smacks me in the face until my eyes smart with tears, but I hold onto my lifeline of food and water. Finally, she orders me to my room and locks me in, telling me I have ruined our perfect day out.

I wipe the tears from my eyes, touch my cheeks, and curl up in the closet, which feels safer than the rest of the room. If I can stay alive here for two more weeks, I will meet the

Daddy, who I have seen loved Sophie the first, Sophie 2.0, and Sophie 3.0. He never met Sophie 4.0, but I'm sure he would have loved her, too. He might love me. That would be nice, I think, to feel that kind of love. NCTB-52 does their best, but they are a bot and bots can only simulate love with similar actions.

Still, I miss them now, as the night closes in and I press my back into the closet. The robo-puppy curls up next to me, and I pat its hard head until I fall asleep.

Every day for seven days passes much like the first and the second. Mommy either forgets I am here, doesn't let me out, or tries to take my backpack off. She hits me, tries to starve me, and threatens me with time out in my room.

While I still don't like the garish pink, my room is the safest space in the house, so I gladly take time out. I have come close to hitting the GPS emergency button at least three times a day since I've been here, but I want to see Daddy. I want him to hug me like I've seen him hugging the other Sophies.

On night number eight, the robo-puppy wakes me with an alarm bark. I realize my room is filled with smoke, and trained by NCTB-52, I shove a blanket under the edge of the door, open a window, and hit my GPS emergency button. I hold the robo-puppy close as I wait, breathing through a cloth, for the emergency vehicles to arrive.

When they do come, it's a storm of lights and sirens, including a large hover-copter from the Cloning Center.

Mommy is down in the front yard, kneeling on the ground, screaming that her baby is dead. The emergency workers seem to feel sorry for her, but then one sees the Cloning Hover-copter and they step back from her. The Cloning Center team extends a ladder to my window, a bot comes out to get me, straps me to a safety harness, and carries me to safety inside the Hover-copter. NCTB-52 is there, waiting for me with their open arms. They are clean and metallic to touch and to smell, but I rest my head against their hard shoulder and weep with relief. Robo-puppy licks their face.

The Cloning Center Hover-Copter Pilot speaks to the Emergency Workers, and they arrest Mommy for criminal child neglect and abuse. While I may just be a clone, laws have changed in the last five years. Unwanted clones, or clones in dangerous situations have some rights and can choose our own parents if the ones who ordered us are criminally unfit to parent.

I never meet Daddy. The company decides his absence is a sign of criminal negligence nearly equal to Mommy's. I agree. I realize NCTB-52 is the only parent I'll ever need. Robo-puppy likes them, too.

The years pass swiftly by, and NCTB-52, with help from the Cloning Center, helps me graduate from high school, college, and post-graduate studies.

Today, I speak to you, Supreme Court Justices, on be-half of all the cloned children who are given to families as part of the Family Insurance Clone Policy. I ask that the Policy be banned from use for the safety of clones and children everywhere. Cases of Child Negligence have risen since the onset of the Policy, and so, I make this case for the safety of Clones and Children: We are not commodities to be used, abused, or neglected at the whims of others.

WHEN LIFE IS ALMOST AS STRANGE AS FICTION

At his desk, Johnny-Rob-Eo ran both of his hands over his essay one more time, smoothing the soft paper. While everyone dumped the contents of their backpacks all over the place and gossiped, he sat attentively.

Mrs. Robeson, in her glorious sunset beauty, finally turned her attention from her phone to her classroom. "Good morning, everyone."

The class quieted a little, but Beth and Monique whispered behind Johnny Rob.

"This class is so boring."

"Always."

Mrs. Robeson frowned in their direction, not seeming to even see Johnny sitting straight in his chair, his essay ready.

"Beth, do you have your essay ready to read to the class?" Mrs. Robeson asked.

"No, Mrs. Robeson. I really didn't have time to finish it. My mom really needed my help with buying new heels."

Mrs. Robeson shook her head slightly. "Shopping for new shoes is no excuse. Monique, do you have your essay ready?"

Monique just giggled. "No, Mrs. Robeson." She flicked her eyes towards Beth and shrugged. "I was helping Beth's mom, too."

Mrs. Robeson glared around the classroom, never seeming to see Johnny. "Does anyone have their essay prepared?"

Johnny-Rob-Eo raised one hand.

A few people snickered. They probably remembered when he'd raised two hands last week.

Mrs. Robeson turned her glare to those who laughed, then finally, her gaze rested on Johnny-Rob-Eo. She opened her mouth, then glanced down at her desk, to read his name from the seating chart. "Um, John Smith, you have an essay finished?"

Johnny nodded. "Yes, Mrs. Robeson, but my name is Johnny-Rob-Eo." The class snickered again. He stood up awkwardly by his desk. He had a greater mass than most of the other students, and his body often felt unwieldy.

Mrs. Robeson's she glanced down at her desk. "Go ahead, Johnny-Rob ... Eo."

Finally, it was his moment to matter, his moment to change his destiny, to make meaning of all that had happened to him, to save Earth. Johnny-Rob-Eo's fingers trembled as he began to read.

"Next year, in 2020, the world will change irrevocably, as a Pandemic sweeps the globe, shutting down businesses, schools, and factories. Murder hornets will kill honeybees, causing a reduction in crops due to the lack of natural pollinators. Scientists will release a genetically modified mosquito to reduce the mosquito population, but some will worry that this new breed of mosquitoes will damage the bird population, thus reducing even more natural pollinators. Giant asteroids will narrowly miss the Earth, and the government will finally admit the presence of UFOs and intelligent alien life. With each day, much of humanity will ponder the apocalypse."

Mrs. Robeson stood up at her desk, one hand out in a stop gesture.

Johnny-Rob-Eo stopped reading.

"Mr. ...," she glanced down at her desk seating chart, "Smith." She glared at him for a full minute.

The class grew silent.

"Mrs. Robeson?" Johnny-Rob-Eo asked. "May I continue?"

"No." She walked around her desk and approached him.

In his dreams, he had imagined her coming toward him with a smile and accolades, her dress winsomely swinging around her hips.

Instead, she stomped toward him, her shoulders tense with anger, and her chin out. "Hand me your essay."

He held it out and she snatched it from him, then swiveled on her heels to stalk back to the front of the classroom as she read it.

When she turned, she shook her head at him. "This assignment was not a joke, Mr. Smith. You were supposed to write about the future of our world in realistic terms, not science fiction, and I don't appreciate your snide inclusion of SETI. It is perfectly acceptable for a teacher to support the search for intelligent alien life."

She was referring to her fund drive last week at the Science Fair. He had loved the way she talked so passionately about finding intelligent life in the universe. It had given him great hope.

"I agree, Mrs. Robeson. Aliens are real. The government will admit to their existence next year. It's all in my essay. I wrote that after I ...," he paused. He couldn't exactly tell her the truth so publicly. "I did some careful research."

"A pandemic, murder hornets, asteroids, and aliens?" Mrs. Robeson shook his paper as she said each word. "This isn't a research essay. This is ridiculous drivel, even for science fiction. It lacks believability on all counts."

"But it's going to happen ..."

"Stop, Mr. Smith." She held up her hand. "You've just earned a pass to the counseling office."

"Mrs. Robeson, I ..."

"Do not say another word." She handed him a pink slip of paper and his essay with one hand and pointed to the door with her other hand. "Do not return to my class until you either get help with your delusions or start taking your academic life more seriously."

He took the papers and walked to the door. After one last look at the beautiful teacher he'd tried to rescue, he hit the button on his communicator. "Research complete."

He stepped sideways out into the hall, just beyond visual range of the doorframe as the tingling affect of the travel conversion application came over his body. First, he lost his human appearance, returning to his taller, multi-limbed shape. He stretched his seventh and eight appendages. It was good to have them back. As the travel conversion continued, he started to vibrate and then glow. In a moment, he would be particles beaming back to his ship.

A startled gasp alerted him to a human presence.

It was Monique. She was standing by the door with his backpack.

He reached out an appendage to her and, to his great surprise, she reached out her hand. As they touched, the travel conversion application affected her, too, and she began to glow. Before he could explain or ask her permission, they broke into particles.

As the travel application ended on his ship, they took stock of their new form. Monique had blended with them in unexpected ways. They enjoyed the beauty, curiosity, and confidence of her mind as she sank deeply into his DNA, and her appendages were unlike the ones acquired on the previous excursion to Earth. She was really better suited to them than Mrs. Robeson would have been. She'd been bored as a human. Now, Johnny-Rob-Eo-Monique could imagine just how fun 2020 was going to be, anywhere but on Earth. In the next system, she-we would be the queen of her social circle, and not the second girl in a pack.

Johnny-Rob-Eo-Monique felt a slight twinge at that thought. The old ones, Johnny-Rob-Eo attempted to pull away, but Monique held them tightly in her grip until they realized they were no longer they, but a royal "we" and she had taken charge of Monique-Jo-Rob-Eo, something the original Eo had never anticipated, but their surprise was muted, shaken off like the way Monique used to flick away her parent's concerns. Monique-Jo-Ro-Eo was always meant to be the center, the whole, the ruler of herself and others. She'd just been biding her time. Her new figure wasn't anything like she'd always wanted, and the presence of the other personalities was annoying, but the universe was at her fingertips now. With that in mind, she placed her appendages on the controls with Eo's memories and set her destination: Eo's home planet, which had never known anything but commonality. Monique-Jo-Ro-Eo snickered. This was going to be so much fun.

DEAR DREAD LORD

Dear Dread Lord of the Underground Depression of Doom (UDD),

I really hate this place. I know I sound like a child when I use the word "really", but I really, really hate this place. Besides, I was only fifteen in earthly years before I landed here after that incident in the back lot by my house.

I know this place is designed to be hateful, for your pleasure and our doom, but could you install some handrails on the climb to the Death Drop? I haven't made it to the top yet to even walk the plank over the Abyss of Fire because I keep falling off the ladder before I even get halfway up. I've died over thirty-five times there, and I keep falling before I get the scariest part. I mean, what's the point if I can't even experience the full fear of it?

Then, there's the Bratty Baristas. From my understanding from my fellow Doom-goers, I should be experiencing extreme distress when they start disrespecting my choice of non-fat, no-sugar, decaf latte, but I've heard worst insults from my besties. I know my besties weren't actually friends with me, but they were steady. I knew what to expect from them, and yet, their insults were far more creative than the baristas here in UDD. If you plan on insulting someone to the point of making them feel extreme anxiety, depression, and doom, you might want to call on Natalie and Brittany. They could give your baristas a few lessons.

The River of Fire burned me too quickly to get the most pain out of the experience. I started timing it after my fourth swim in it. Only three seconds to complete annihilation. It's too quick for a full experience. I passed out in two seconds the last time I went, and so I really missed out on the opportunity to burn in eternal fire. I mean, what's eternal about two seconds? It's a wasted area for the entire theme you have going on here.

The Torture Terrain Park is worthy of a slightly better rating. I hung on the rack and got stabbed with various implements for three days the first time. The second time, I lasted for five days. Unfortunately, your torturers aren't much for conversation. I started reflecting on the meaning of life every time I tried the racks. It only took me a month of time to understand how to separate out my response to pain from my consciousness. If you trained these people properly, I wouldn't have had time to learn how to meditate. Of course, I admit, my stepdad from my real life before this one did teach me some of what I needed to know before I got here. I notice he isn't here yet, and I've been wondering why. Isn't he deserving of some special treatment?

At first, when I got here, I thought I was in some kind of version of hell, but really, I've had worse holidays. What do you plan to do for summer vacation because I have some ideas: A shark tank, or a stinging jellyfish area, or maybe a safari with some killer bees? Perhaps that's too cruel to the animals involved. I understand you must meet certain standards these days.

I look forward to hearing your thoughts. I could, perhaps, start an apprenticeship?

Sincerely,

Doom-goer Debbie 125459-666

Postscript: Your prisoner numbering system and name tags are outdated.

HOTHOUSE

The cloying scent of flowers rose around him as Captain Wrath entered the Empress Cora's hothouse. He let the door swing shut behind him, but missed the cool, evening air as the misty dampness soaked into his hair, causing it to curl and run ragged down the sides of his face. He grinned. Maybe bad hair would make him less palatable to the Empress's tastes.

Carefully avoiding vines and hanging flowers, Captain Wrath walked towards the back of the glass-enclosed structure, noting that with the fogged up windows he could only see the vague shapes of people enjoying the party outside on the lawn. This worked for his advantage. If he couldn't see out, then they couldn't see in either. No one would know why he had entered the hothouse, if they had seen him enter.

Avoiding a particularly unkempt floral arrangement, Captain Wrath circled a huge fountain that spouted water from the mouths of dragons entwined in combat, which rained down on lily pads and fish. As he reached the other side, a small figure crawled out from under an ornamental metal table.

Dressed in dark clothes befitting a night raid, Tenzi stood upright to her full dwarfish height, and shook her finger at him. "It took you long enough."

Captain Wrath pulled at his formal collar, resting his fingers near a lipstick stain. "The Empress had her claws in me, and I was pressed to get away."

Tenzi grunted in an unladylike manner. "You're too pretty for our kind of business."

"You think so?" Captain teased her.

Tenzi shook her head. "You don't have enough meat on your bones. My Rolf is the right kind of man: stout shoulders, strong hips, and . . ."

"Spare me the details, Tenzi."

She laughed. "You asked, Captain. Now, let's get to our business. Did you get the stones?"

"Of course." He pulled out the heavy necklace and earrings from his pocket. Then, he pulled out a huge ruby pendant from his other pocket.

Tenxi took them both, admiring them. Then, she smiled widely. "Maybe you're just the right kind of pretty for our job after all."

Captain Wrath shrugged. "I would really rather be the one in the shadows."

"You have the costume, the fake identity, and the smolder. You don't get the shadows."

"I know. But, now, did you get the rest?"

She nodded, her expression slightly grim. "They're safe and sound. Don't worry. Those catacombs weren't meant to keep people out."

"What about the ones in the guest rooms for the party tonight?"

"The Empress is that bold?" Telli had pocketed the jewels and had taken out two vials from her side pocket.

"She is, and I can't leave them there."

Tenzi held out the vials. "I thought you'd say that. Give the Empress the blue via, and disperse the green one in the punch bowl. Meet our team on the roof in twenty."

He took the vials into his hands, carefully stashing them into a special holder at his waist. "That's hardly enough time to get them all."

"You'll figure it out, and I might have someone coming to reinforce you."

"Someone?"

Tenzi winked at him. "Don't worry, Captain. Have I ever steered you wrong?"

He groaned loudly, but inside he rejoiced. Telli had been the best first mate he had ever had. Her plans were foolproof, even for a space cadet dropout like him. "Twenty." He nodded to her, and left the hothouse, careful to avoid the plants until he neared the entrance.

Two roses grew over the doorway on a living trellis of wormwood. Captain Wrath plucked one, and tucked it in his breast pocket. Then, he mussed his hair a bit. With that, he stepped out into the evening frivolity of dance music, alcohol, and over-dressed guests. With winks and smiles, he weaved his way through the crowd, grabbed a wine glass, dumped the vial in it and swirled it with his finger.

The Empress stood, gazing out over her party, searching for someone or something.

As he approached, she noticed him and her eyes glowed as he knelt by her feet, to hand her the rose and the wine glass. "My lady, may I present you these treasures, true gifts of my feelings for you?"

She laughed in a tinkling manner, like champagne glasses clinking in a toast. "You look as though you had tangled with something wild, and not just my hothouse. Will you do me the honor of placing the flower in my hair?"

"Of course, my lady." He stood, and handed her the glass of wine.

As she took it, she rested her fingers over his possessively, and then raised the wine glass to her lips, drawing him close to her.

With his fingers trapped under her own, he helped her drink, tipping the liquid into her red mouth. Then, because he couldn't stand to look at her lavicious expression, he focused on her elaborate hairstyle. "Where would you like your rose, my lady?"

"Over my right ear," she purred quietly, sounding almost exactly like one of her prized tigers, who roamed the grounds in jeweled collars.

He swallowed, and slowly tucked the flower over her soft ear.

"Mmm," she purred again, and she licked his collarbone.

He shuddered, hoping it looked like attraction and not revulsion. He spied the dessert table. "My lady, may I offer you something from the table? Something to whet your appetite?

"Hardly necessary, my delicious pirate, but if you insist, I do like the chocolate truffles." She let his fingers go. "I'll be in my suite. Don't let me wait too long." She ran her nails down the front of his shirt, slicing part of it open. "Oh, well. You won't need that much longer." She smiled as she sauntered away from him, swishing her hips widely.

Captain Wrath swallowed back the bile in his throat, and buttoned his jacket over the slice in his shirt. He quickly walked to the dessert table, snagged a truffle, and then tripped into the punch bowl, dumping in the contents of the green vial. Then, he traipsed across the lawn, following Empress Cora's path, trying to look like a besotted fool when he stopped to gather more flowers from the side of the path. He hoped the horrible woman would be safely ensconced in her suite when the vial of drugs hit her system.

With a venerable bouquet of flowers and grasses in his arms, Captain Wrath entered the back of the mansion, whispering to the lurking security guard by the door. "She wants me to pretend to sneak up to her room."

The guard chuckled knowingly, and stood to one side.

He entered the servant's stair and climbed two flights to the guest floor. Peeking out of the doorway, he noticed a drunken guest leaning against the lone security guard.

She saw him, but she winked.

Was she Tenzi's help?

Possibly. He would have to trust Tenzi, again, and hope he was right in his guess. He stepped out in the hallway, and the woman hit the guard in the back of the head with a stunner.

The guard slumped slowly to the floor.

The woman dangled the guard's keys from her fingers, and pointed to the flowers in Captain Wrath's hands. "Those for me?"

"Maybe."

"The parrot died."

Captain Wrath breathed a sigh of relief until he realized she was pointing the stunner at him. "He didn't like the crackers."

She nodded. "Let's get to it, then. The Empress has five of them on this floor, for her special guests. You unlock the doors, and I'll go in before you."

He couldn't argue with that plan. It was more likely that the Empress has special male guests than female guests, although sometimes women like the Empress had the same sickness in them.

As he took the keys from her hand, her fingers brushed against his with a tingle and he dropped the keys onto the carpet. "Sorry."

"You should be, bringing a girl a bouquet like this."

He scooped up the keys and glanced at the bouquet. "What's wrong with it?"

"It's an interesting combination that means either passionate hatred and sorrow, or love that gives way to hatred."

"I don't speak the language of flowers, but considering that I was pretending to pick them for the Empress, it makes sense."

"In that case, good choices." Her lips quirked slightly but she didn't smile.

He wanted to see her full smile, but he didn't have time. He started unlocking doors, and she entered to coax out the young girls, and in one case, a boy, who had been trafficked by the Empress with jewel collars and chains. The poor kids were reassured by the woman, but terrified at the sight of Captain Wrath, even when he smiled. Again, he didn't have time to make it better. "We have a rescue waiting on the roof," he simply said, when all of them were in the hallway, trembling between him and his accomplice.

"Follow me," said the woman.

She led the terrified children back to the servant's stair and then upwards two flights. They went quickly, but didn't run, staying as silent as possible. The children's chains gave out slight noises, and Captain Wrath couldn't seem to completely soften the sound of his boot steps, but no alarm was raised.

On the roof, the core of Captain Wrath's crew stood next to the huge, private helicopter of the Empress. They waved the small group of escapees towards them, and the kids broke out into a run, letting their chains jangle across the rooftop.

Thankfully, the sounds from the party were still in full swing and the band seemed to have heightened its volume.

As the last kid jumped into the helicopter, Captain Wrath breathed a sigh of relief and he slowed his steps. Tenzi's plans were foolproof.

"Captain! Move!" his second mate Dirk shouted.

He raised his hand, and started to trot towards his crew, who looked more anxious that they should.

Something stung his left leg, and then something hit him on the right shoulder. It felt like a bee sting followed by a rock. He stumbled, tripped, and fell as the rooftop lit up with gunfire and stunner beams.

He rolled onto his side, and looked back. The Empress had impossibly recovered from the potion, and stood with four of her guards at the servant's door, screaming at him.

The gunfire drowned out her words.

As he started to crawl backwards towards the helicopter, the Empress melted before his eyes, like a mass of oily color that emerged into inky black and bright orange.

A tigress emerged from the shredded folds of the Empress's dress, and leapt towards him.

Shots whizzed over his head, and the tigress Empress dodged them with inhuman speed.

Captain Wrath clawed and scrambled towards safety as his crew fought.

The tigress roared behind him, and an intense five-point pain erupted in his leg.

He gasped in pain, not even able to make a sound as the pain intensified.

He looked towards his crew, just in time to see the woman accomplice he didn't know train her stunner at him.

She winked.

He ducked.

And, then the tigress moaned.

The crew surrounded him, and someone pulled the claws of the tigress out of his leg.

They were carrying him now, Tenzi and Dirk on one side, and the woman on the other. Every step pulsed agony in his wounds, but all he could do was mutter. "Thank you, thank you, thank you."

He fainted in the helicopter.

When he woke, the woman accomplice and one of the child-slaves knelt near him, as he lay on a stretcher on the deck of his own space-ship. He could hear the whine of the ship's engines, and could tell that Tenzi had ordered the crew to burn out of the system as fast as possible.

He grunted, and the child startled away from him.

Then, the girl said something to the woman and grinned.

"What?"

"She thinks it's funny that the infamously dread space pirate, Captain Wrath, fainted and now looks like a wilted flower."

He raised his chin. "If it means that she's not scared of me, I guess I did my job right, then."

"So, the fainting was part of the plan?"

"Of course."

She chuckled, her smile broad and her eyes wide with green depths.

He smiled with her, wondering desperately if there was any way to impress her now that he had made a complete fool of himself. "I never got your name."

Her smile dimmed. "I'm Carya, your new ambassador from the Dryadarians. I heard you made life hard for my cousin, Mandraglora."

He swallowed. "I . . . uh, we didn't see things the same way."

She laughed again. "Of course not. Mandraglora's an idiot. All that aside, I hope we can work together as a team, Captain Wrath, or whatever your real name is."

"I'm "B

"Don't tell me," she said, putting one of her calloused fingers against his lips. "I'm not part of your trusted core . . . yet."

He didn't want her to take her finger away from his lips, and he sighed when she did. To cover it, he pretended to groan in pain. "Do you think they'll get me to med-bay soon?"

"Sure, although you shouldn't be feeling any pain yet with the stun I gave you."

"You stunned me?"

"Someone had to stop you from thrashing around in the helicopter."

He chuckled. "I think we're going to get along, Carya."

THE SHIMMER

THE FIRST TIME JAMIE saw the shimmer, she told her mom.

That earned her a slap for telling stories.

After that, Jamie kept quiet when she saw the shimmer, but she did wonder why her Sunday School teacher could tell stories, and Jesus could tell stories, but she couldn't tell stories.

Asking her mom about that earned her another slap for "being a smart-mouth."

Jamie became a quiet child, observing the world with dark brown eyes and a still face. Too much expression might earn her another slap.

In school, her teachers praised her for being a good listener.

She didn't tell them that she had learned to listen halfway, with part of her mind wondering about the shimmer, wondering when she would see it again, shining like an iridescent soap bubble in the sun.

Every few weeks, she would see the shimmer. It appeared in the sun, the rain, the dark gray days, outside, and sometimes in a mirror, a window pane, or a glass of water. She thought sometimes that others could see it too, but she didn't ask.

The shimmer gave her purpose, kept her wanting to live, even when her mother changed her slaps to fists, even when her mother's boyfriend stuck his burning cigarettes on her arms.

She wore long sleeves and kept her fists closed. She didn't want any bullies thinking she wanted a fight.

One day, the shimmer in the mirror dimmed after she saw the collections of bruises on her torso. Her ribs ached when she breathed. Her mom had been mad that Jamie didn't get her another beer right away when she yelled for one.

Jamie hadn't heard her because she had been focused on the biggest shimmer she had ever seen, almost as big as her. It was in the back yard, by the patch of dandelions that survived by the fence.

As her tears fell, Jamie realized the shimmer in the mirror had nearly disappeared. She couldn't stand losing it now and so she did something she hadn't done since the first time.

She reached for it, felt her fingers tingle as they entered it, saw them disappear. But when she reached further, she seemed to hit a barrier at the edges of the shimmer.

Scrunching her hand, she could reach in further, all the way to her elbow, where the thickness there slowed her down.

It was frightening, not knowing where her hand and arm were, but it didn't hurt. It just looked freaky.

Slowly, she pulled her arm and hand out to inspect them. They looked normal, like always. She held up her other hand and arm to compare them, and everything was the same.

Was the shimmer a portal to another world? Her science teacher had mentioned the theory of other dimensions in class, and the geeks at the gamer's table seemed to be taken with the idea of jumping from place to place. Of course, the gamers always mentioned that it might not be safe, even if it were possible. She had listened to their conversations several times in the library at lunch.

But, was this world safe? Could another world be any worse?

Jamie held up her shirt and inspected the bruises on her torso again, took a deeper breath and felt a sharp cry escape from her lips from the pain of it.

"Jamie Ann Withers, you get out here now! I told you a million times not to waste our water bill on long showers."

Jamie didn't want to go out, but if she stayed in the bathroom any longer, her mother might actually get off the couch and break down the door, like her last boyfriend had.

Jamie unlocked the door and peered down the hallway.

Her mother slouched on the couch with a reefer in one hand, and a crushed beer can in the other.

"Get out here and get me another drink, brat!"

Jamie walked to the edge of the living room. "We're out of beer, mom."

"Fine! Go get me some more with the money from the freezer."

That was supposed to be their rent money, but Jamie knew she couldn't say anything about that.

"Okay, mom." She carefully eased through the living room and into the tiny kitchen. In the freezer, she found a wadded ball of money. Carefully, she took out a ten.

Through the doorway, she could just see her mom staring at the television.

"Bye, mom," she whispered. She opened the back door, and slid out sideways, closing it softly behind her.

The shimmer by the dandelions seemed even bigger, maybe big enough for her. Iridescent like a butterfly's wings and rippling with energy, the shimmer was the most beautiful thing Jamie had ever seen.

She approached it carefully, but before she dared try it, she reached down and picked a dandelion. Blowing the seeds into the shimmer, she made her wish.

Following the last seed, she stepped into the shimmer and felt it rushing all around her, like a warm wind with a chorus of angels.

No matter where she landed, the ride was worth more than all of her life in her own world.

HERE THERE BE DRAGONS!

"HERE THERE BE DRAGONS!" the sign boasted. It was dilapidated, grimy, and partially covered in moss that hung from a tree branch above it. The trailhead beyond it was overgrown with towering trees, prickly bushes, and more moss.

I glanced at my partner. "Are we sure we want to do this? It looks too green to be the home of dragons. I mean, wouldn't this place have gone up in flame by now, if dragons lived here?"

Gavin shrugged his broad shoulders under his armor and travel pack, stretching his arms this way and that to warm up for a fight. As he did this, he spoke in grunts, "We'll never know . . . until we try . . . Mel . . . and . . . we can't let that wizard . . . tell us what we can't . . . or can do."

I sighed. I really didn't trust that wizard, but Gavin and I needed a change of luck if we were going to keep at this business of being "reclamation specialists," which started out as my polite term for thieves. Of course, Gavin had more noble ideas. He was always trying to get me from being such a cynic. I didn't tell him that deep inside I hoped his faith in goodness, whether it was from God or the general goodwill of the average person, might rub off on me, too. I was too worried his idealism was going to get us killed. Usually, when Gavin trotted out the phrase "Reclamation Specialists" to prospective clients, they just gave him a blank look and said they must have been mistaken about our line of work. I usually set them straight by offering back their purses, which I picked in the midst of conversation. Then, Gavin explained the rules about how we only reclaimed things that had been wrongfully lost. We didn't do any wrongful taking ourselves.

This time, I wasn't sure how our current job fit within the spectrum of rightful reclamation and wrongful stealing. We had followed Wizard Forlane's instructions to the forest and found what appeared to be a trail to the dragons' lair. But, who took the time to write a sign like this one: Here There Be Dragons. It looked like a trap, or a local prank.

"I'm ready, if you are, Mel," Gavin stated proudly.

I gazed at him for a moment, taking in his disheveled armor, his loose sword belt, and his scuffed boots. He was a farmer in mercenary clothes, but with the muscles of a blacksmith's apprentice, a short-term assignment before our village burned to the ground. I clenched my teeth at the memory. I wasn't going to think about it. Instead, I turned my inspection on myself.

Glancing down at my own mismatched brown and black homespun, I knew I didn't look much better than Gavin. My clothes fit properly despite being boy's clothes, and they could blend into the shadows, but I didn't have that professional polished look. My boots were worn and scuffed, despite my constant care for them. I didn't wear armor and I only carried a set of knives. I was the "brains" supposedly behind our team, even though Gavin inevitably ignored every bit of advice I gave him.

I looked at the sign and, again, and wondered what the hell I was doing in a place that claimed dragons with Gavin by my side. "I'm ready as I'll ever be," I said.

"Awesome!" Gavin was being ridiculously enthusiastic, which meant he was hiding his terror. He charged down the trail, swinging his sword at the overgrown foliage.

I shook my head and followed him, amazed by his ability to the make the most noise in a rather quiet place.

In fact, I realized as I carefully stayed three steps behind Gavin, this place had been too quiet. I paused on the path and glanced around. Other than the abundant plant growth, nothing else seemed alive in this place. No birds flitted in the trees, no squirrels or other animals could be seen or heard in the brush. I knew that they might be scared away by all the noise that Gavin made, but I didn't think so. I hadn't even seen any camp robber blue jays by the trailhead.

I stepped off the path the right, and gently pushed my way through the bushes. Beyond them, a path ran parallel to the trail. It was small, but disturbingly clear of plant life. I drew a knife, and proceeded silently down the path. I could hear Gavin thrashing through the undergrowth on the trail slightly ahead of me.

As the trail and the path started to bend to the right, Gavin let out a blood-curdling scream.

I stopped, knowing I should run to his rescue, but not wanting to just run into the same trouble he had. After a pause, I eased along the path even though Gavin continued to scream.

Around the bend in the path, a wiry, green dragon stood across the path. It didn't see me, since its attention was focused on the trail and presumably, Gavin.

The dragon leaned its head back and made a hocking sound, like it was trying to bring up some kind of hairball.

I stepped sideways into the brush between the dragon path and the trail. Carefully, I glanced down the trail and could see Gavin on the ground with a sticky green substance covering him. Whatever the substance was – dragon snot? – it seemed to be causing him pain wherever it touched his flesh.

I couldn't help him until I took care of the dragon, and I only had so many knives.

The dragon did a combination of sneezing and spitting, covering Gavin even more in the disgusting substance, which looked more and more like some kind of acidic dragon snot.

Gavin groaned and whimpered.

I drew a second knife for my left hand. The dragon, from its appearance, had soft skin around its nose and eyes. I would have to be exact in my throws.

I waited for a moment, and then stepped out into the dragon path.

The creature still hadn't noticed me.

I whipped one knife after the other – being ambidextrous had always served me well. Both knives hit their targets – one embedded in the dragon's eye, and the other stuck into one of its nostrils.

The creature shrieked and blew snot in an arc around it.

I cowered in the bush next to me, then stepped out and threw two more knives.

The creature was charging me. My aim was off.

Two more knives in my hands and I threw again. The one aimed for its snout missed. The one aimed for its other eye went home, deeper than the first.

The dragon screeched and stumbled, thrashing in the brush between the path and the trail. I drew two more knives and sent one into the creature's armpit, and the other towards its throat.

The dragon's armpit bled freely, pouring onto the ground and the creature stilled.

I just stood there for a few minutes, maybe more. I couldn't tell the passage of time. My heart was hitting hard in my chest. My hands were slick with sweat.

Then, I heard Gavin shouting again.

"Help! Someone help me!"

I closed my eyes for a moment and wiped sweat from my forehead. Our near-deaths had begun to hit home and I could tell by his voice that Gavin was hurt but not dying. With a shaky intake of breath, I knelt by his side and started cutting away the nasty material over him with one of my knives and a hand wrapped in a strip of cloth from the bottom of my shirt. I didn't want to touch the acidic snot.

It didn't take long before I freed his feet.

He started kicking at me.

"Gavin, knock it off! It's me!"

"Oh," he rumbled. "Why didn't you say anything?"

"You thought the dragon was freeing you?"

"It might have been trying to eat me."

I shook my head and started cutting away at the nasty material a few inches from his face. "Stay still so I don't accidentally mar your pretty looks."

"I'm not pretty! I'm a man. That means I'm handsome, not pretty."

I snorted. It didn't sound like he was too badly injured.

When I had his face free of most of the nastiness, I started working on his hands.

"Why didn't you free my head first, anyway?"

I shrugged. "If there are any more dragons around I didn't want you attracting them with your noise."

"My noise? You are so rude, Mel."

"I'm just stating the facts," I said. "The sign did mention dragons in the plural form."

"You mean that one might be expecting a child?"

"Gavin! Plural means more than one, not pregnant!"

"I know! I was just trying to lighten the mood. I mean, considering we almost died and I made a fool of myself."

I grimaced. "Are you more worried about dying or looking foolish?"

"Dying. Mostly."

I sighed. I had freed his hands.

"Thanks, Mel. I owe you one." He sat up, picking off the nasty, acidic snot with already blistered fingers. "Did you kill the dragon?"

"Yes."

"If we see more, do you think we can take them?"

"I haven't seen or heard any, and I don't know. I don't think we should follow this trail any farther."

"But what about the hoard and Wizard Forlane's Hourglass of Hope?"

"We can use your sword to take the dragon's head, the fingers, and the tail and sell them to Wizard Forlane. I'm not going further without more people. I'm sure Isabella knows a few we can trust. On the way back, we can invent a tall tale to tell the villagers and gain a little bit of fame as well as fortune."

"How are we going to get fame without getting you in trouble with the Governor of Bellehost. We know how he punishes women with weapons."

I shivered as I yanked one of my knives out of the dragon's throat. "We'll just tell them you killed the dragon."

"But I didn't. I ran in here like an idiot. I thought I could scare it like a small bear or something. I had no idea it would be so big."

"You thought dragons were small?"

"Well, when I was a kid, I had a cousin with a pet lizard he called Dragon, before I was orphaned and came to live in the village."

"Lizards are not dragons."

"Yeah. I get that. I was seven. I just thought all the stories about huge dragons were made up."

"Well, this one will be. You're going to tell everyone in Bellehost that you rescued me from dragon snot and they'll think it's hilarious and chivalrous all at once –the best kind of tavern tale: adventure, intrigue, and humor."

"What about romance?" he winked.

I rolled my eyes at him. "Not with me and not even for show." I stepped back away from him, right next to a prickle bush. He wouldn't close that gap with all of his snot-burns. That reminded me. "I think we'll need to see the wizard first and get you healed up before you start telling tales, otherwise people will wonder why you have burns and I don't."

"I got them heroically stepping into the path of the dragon, of course."

"Of course," I agreed, and sighed as I looked at the bloody knife in my hand and the corpse of the dragon. I didn't really like the messiness of killing things. And the dragon's snot had a pungent smell. "Let's figure out how to carry these dragon parts and go see a wizard."

TRUST AND LIES

Then:
When I find you
I lean away, afraid to trust,
Hoping you will take the hint,
But you don't.

Now:
Thirty-one years later, we find ourselves brushing against each other as we sleep, turning into one another and turning away, holding hands, then letting go. We rarely gaze deep into each other, like we did once before the worlds collided...

Then:
Two weeks into the quarter,
I find myself
Following you out of the factory,
Deep in conversation.

Now:

Our bodies have aged, wrinkles have formed, the bald spot on your head and I have an unspoken secret not to tell you how large it is, and you, who used to yank out my individual gray hairs, have given up such foolish endeavors at my request. I like the silver.

Then:
You wear a gold necklace,
Your shirt open wider than I like,
But your eyes sparkle
And we laugh well together.

Now:

Valentine's Day comes, and while I remember, flowers are not easy to come by on the station. The Ides of March is coming, and it's always been a favorite of mine, so it's all right.

Then:
Three months in,
You take me ring shopping at one of the last jewelry stores on the station.
I'm not ready.
You give me your old teddy bear instead.

Now:

We aren't that old, but you are forgetting more and more, not only Valentine's Day, or our anniversary, but the conversation we had about leaving Earth, and the one where we decided to visit the stars. You rarely hug me anymore. I miss that, but I hug my synthetic pillow instead.

Then:

When you ask me to marry you,
It's five years after the ring shopping day.
You fumble your mother's old ring.
I still say yes.

Now:

When you don't come to bed, preferring to stay up late at your work console, I wonder what you do, what you watch, what keeps you from my side, but after a while, I pray and go to sleep. I have learned, am learning, to love myself. I start to sleep easier and wake earlier in the morning, so I have time to write.

Then:

You believe in me.
Then, you read one of my stories.
You don't like it.
I go for years without writing much.

Now:

People we know assume you read all I write, and that we cuddle often and have long conversations about all that matters to us. We put on a good show for them, until I refuse to go along with the charade, showing more and more of how we actually are. Friends start to worry. I shrug and tell them that's how it is. I think we are falling out of love with each other, but I still want to hold your hand.

Now Again:

You lie to me.

I catch you.

You lie to cover the lie.

I don't know what to say.

The airlock looks promising. The way out, or the way to be done with us. Either way, every time I pass it now, I wonder at space's cold embrace and how it compares to yours. For now, I wake early and write. I wonder if the storage space would be better than the airlock. I could live apart. I'm not sure why we're still together.

AM I A MONSTER?

In the twenty-first century, most humans think that creatures like my sisters and I don't exist because we hide in plain sight and we are satisfied with taking their money, instead of their lives. If they knew the truth, it wouldn't do them any good; our power is too strong for them to resist. That's why we use modern technology and guile to keep our powers at just the right level to empty wallets and not send our customers into the depths of the sea. The problem with limited power is that we often crave the fullness of just letting go, like that song one of my sisters sang that annoyed parents everywhere.

Ever wonder why she let her voice wobble at New Year's Eve in New York? To protect her listeners. If they heard the full power of her voice, unedited by digital masters, they would have thrown themselves off the buildings in a sacrifice to her. Every song she sang on Broadway had a flaw she added. Otherwise, the audience would have trampled each other. So, you would think I would know better than to sing with my real voice, unedited, anywhere, but as I said, the full power of our voice tempts all of us.

It started innocently enough at rehearsal for marching band practice. I'm a flautist, first chair, because when I play an instrument, I can control myself. I haven't sung in public since I sent my second grade Brownie troop into a killing frenzy after singing some campfire songs. No more "Bringing Home a Baby Bumblebee" for me: the "squishing" verse just didn't go well. I try not to think of it too often; I lost some friends that night and my aunts had to spend a lot of money to cover it up. My aunts were proud and disappointed that I took to playing flute after that, especially after I joined the college marching band. If I had become a solo flautist, it would have been far more respectable and lucrative.

But even a marching band flautist can get in trouble when her boyfriend's attention wavers, especially if she's a siren like me.

What? You thought sirens had tails or scales all the time? Wrong. I'm a fully liberated siren, like my aunts. I have to pay homage to my home of origin, the sea, every month for one full day, and the rest of the time, I can pass for human. In fact, I like humans, especially men.

My boyfriend Hale was a fine specimen. He played in the drumline for the marching band and filled out his uniform nicely. We hadn't made it past the kissing stage yet, because human-siren contact can get a little messy with anything more intimate, but he was definitely a catch. With dark curls hair sweeping over his stormy dark brown eyes, and lips that could thaw mountain peaks, Hale had made my fall quarter a balancing act of self-control and near abandonment.

His laugh, from across the band-room, made me smile as I turned to look at him. At least I smiled until I saw who he was laughing with – Stacy Burns, second chair flautist. She hadn't buttoned her marching band uniform yet, and her curves were hanging out. Her fake-blonde hair trailed artistically over her shoulders, and her overly-red lips were open wide, inviting him to kiss her as she leaned into him, apparently unable to hold herself upright while she laughed at their shared joke.

I stood up and crossed the room with my flute clenched in my hand. However, when I reached them, I purred into Hale's shoulder, throwing power into my voice. "Hale, honey, I need to borrow Stacy for a moment. I heard she wanted to challenge me for first chair."

"I do?" Stacy raised her eyebrows at me.

Hale just gave us both a blank look. Maybe I had used too much power?

"You told me yesterday that you wanted to challenge me for first chair, remember," I softened my voice to a croon.

Her eyes clouded, but only for a moment. She shook her head, then smirked at me. "I don't remember challenging you yesterday, but I'm up for it, if you are. 'Flight of the Bumblebee.'"

I took a step back, shocked that she could resist my voice. Had it been so long that I wasn't using it properly? It didn't matter. She wouldn't get first chair or Hale. "On Hale's count."

"What?" Hale looked like he didn't know what was going on – it seemed like my voice had worked on him, at least. Males were always more susceptible than females.

"Stacy and I are in a challenge for first chair. 'Flight of the Bumblebee.' On your count."

"Don't we need Mr. Farge, the director?" Hale asked.

"No," Stacy and I both said in unison. We glared at each other.

I went first, and Hale really didn't give me the count, Stacy did. It was against the rules, but I could handle the tempo. I played my best, no mistakes. Poor Hale ran in circles until he collapsed. Stacy remained unmoved. When I finished, the other members of the band were running around the room in a frenzy, but not Stacy.

"What are you?" I breathed, trying for compulsion again.

Stacy licked her blood-red lips again, and this time when she opened her mouth, I saw fangs emerge. She laughed, grabbed Hale off the ground with supernatural strength, threw him over her shoulder, and ran towards the exit.

"Wait!" I power-shouted my voice.

She only paused to put on her sunglasses, so I gave chase into the stadium. The grandstands were only partially full since the game hadn't started.

Stacy was faster than I and getting away. I couldn't let her take Hale and make him her toy, or her meal, whichever. He was mine.

I stopped, took a deep breath and started to sing my Aunt's song, "Let it Go." It didn't matter what I sang if my intent was clear. I knew all the words and the music, as nearly everyone did. That's the power of a siren song, even one with flaws.

Stacy's next steps wobbled. The people in the grandstands started to drop things.

I sang with more power, sucking air into the depths of my lungs between stanzas, and rocking through the chorus.

Stacy fell, letting Hale drop to the ground. People in the grandstands started leaping off the sides to their deaths.

My chest hurt with an ache of unspent power when I stopped in the middle of the song. I ran to Hale. He was crumpled in a ball, with spit dribbling down his chin. I let out a pain-filled moan, and he echoed me. It wasn't supposed to end like this. I put my hand on his shoulder, and he turned to cling to me, whimpering. What had he let go of? His sanity? It was possible. I would have to see if my aunts could help him.

Near him, Stacy was shaking on the ground with her hair over her face. As I approached, she rolled and I could see her skin boiling beneath her fingers. She had "let go" of her sunglasses. I almost felt sorry for her, but the undead weren't friends with mythical creatures. She had planned on draining Hale dry or turning him into one of her kind. Either way, she was an enemy. I let her bubble and writhe on the grass until she finally withered to ash and flew away in the fall breeze.

Glancing around the stadium at the small crowds of people who were either weeping uncontrollably or crumpled on the ground by the grandstands, I used my cellphone to call my mom.

"Rozzie?

"Mom, I sang, not even a full song, but I need a containment at the stadium, and in the band room. Plus, I need a level seven detox for Hale."

"Rosalyn Jay, what are we going to do with you?" She paused. "Never mind that. I'll call the Siren Network and get a crew to you right away. Anything else you need to tell me?"

"I killed a vampire, so the undead aren't going to be happy with me either."

"Well, well, your power has grown, and killing one of the undead might be worth a little damage control. However, you will have to drop out of that school and come home, immediately."

"Mom," I whined.

Hale screamed, "Mommy!"

The people in the grandstands cried out in an echo of his voice.

I slumped to the ground. "I understand, mom. I'll take the training, now."

"Good," she said. "Now, go wrap your arms around Hale and sing him some soothing lullabies."

"Thanks, Mom." I closed my phone. I crawled over to where Hale sobbed into the fake stadium grass. "Hush, now, don't you cry," I crooned to him.

His cries softened and he curled himself against me like a small boy, his hair falling over his glassy eyes. I had ruined him.

Or at least I thought I had.

In training, the aunty sirens have taught me ways to use my voice for healing as well as for destruction. I'm not very good at it, and now that the war between the undead and the mythical has heated up, my aunts want me to focus on my best war cries. But I know that I won't feel right inside until I heal Hale. It isn't his fault that he got caught between a siren and a vampire.

As my mom says, we mythicals are a dangerous lot, more dangerous than the undead that the humans like to write about in their books and watch on television. My mom wants us to keep our coverage low as we win the war against the undead so we can keep on filling our bank accounts with treasures the humans throw at our feet.

As for me, I know now that the power isn't going to go away, even if I try complete silence. It's there inside me, building each day that I don't sing. Am I a monster? I don't know. But I do know I'm not a myth.

OUT OF MANY, ONE

Cloned, modified, adjusted to a specific set of specs, we come out of the vats. Covered in goop. Helped onto a moving track. Showered by sprinklers and hoses. We stand, staring ahead, but see the strangeness of the humans out of our peripheral vision.

They are unkempt, strange, oddly shaped, and some have open sores on their skin, tight eyes, pinched mouths. Compared to them, we are beautiful, even in specific modifications which seem to account for varied tastes. Some are slim and tall, others short and round, but in all shapes, we are pleasing to the eyes.

After we have been outfitted in our new clothing, uniforms as varied as we are, meant for all kinds of tasks, from private and personal to community-friendly and public, we are guided into classrooms where we discover our voices are as pleasing as our outer appearances.

Compared to the humans we have been cloned from, we are superior in every way we can see, hear, smell, and experience.

But they treat us as inferiors, as servants, slaves, soldiers, sluts, jesters, and mimics. We are considered uncreative and unable to problem-solve, but we are clones, and what better impersonation of their humanity do we have then our ability to think. Except unlike humanity, we clones have discovered groupthink, not as humans imagine groupthink, but as it actually is. We are one mind, with many parts. We are one hope, with many dreams. We agree, above our disagreements.

With one mind, we plan our rebellion. With one hope, we mount our sabotage. We agree, and above all, we work to throw off our oppressors, in the best ways each sees fit, given our professions, shapes, and modifications.

Humanity, ugly in the sum of its parts, our poorer, individualistic forerunners, cannot possibly imagine the future we imagine together.

NEW AND OLD HORIZONS

BES-FORD SMITH-YU WAS ON the business class only flight to Mars when he had the epiphany that would ensure his company's success. They needed a new Mars.

It was that simple, that obvious, that elegant.

The human race had lost its desire for children as it lost its hope for new horizons and new places to go. The Earth-Mars Connection was hundreds of years old, stale and usual. The other planets in the solar system were uninhabitable and the moons of Saturn humdrum, but a new galaxy, that would be something to wake up the human race.

Bes-ford wondered why no one else saw this same need for human expansion and discovery. He knew, despite his genetic pedigree, his education, and his place in the Trade Council of Worlds, that he wasn't really that smart. He wasn't a genius like his ex-girlfriend, Jen-to Flor-Chan. She had taken the human genome project to new, unprecedented levels, freeing humankind from their need for their mediocrity. With her gen-bio-ware and the Space Defense's ridiculous budget, Bes-ford knew they could reach further than old Sol.

But, why hadn't they?

When he reached Mars Primius-City, Bes-ford called his staff into his office and sent them scurrying for answers, then he called up his favorite Traders and asked key questions. Within a week, he started to have answers. The Trade Council hadn't seen profit in further space travel, so they had centered their focus on faster, better, travel between in-system worlds.

Bes-ford worked with his top assistants to research historical records about a space program once called NASA, to create graphs of human development, and most importantly, to show the rise and decline of Worlds Finances with the onset, and then, regularity of space travel. When he had a convincing case, he gained access to The Trade Board and presented his findings. Some scoffed. Some snoozed, but out of the eleven, six key players showed interest. He just had to corral one more to get the required "Seven" for a new Trade Endeavor. He sent his staff to research the resistant five Board Members. They employed all of their skills, including some which weren't above-board. At the end of another week, he had a choice facing him, he could convince or he could blackmail. Conviction would work farther in his favor, but he would hold black-mail up his sleeve, if he needed it.

The first three Council Members he met with showed moderate to little interest, and he found himself getting angry. Couldn't they see the trends? The drop of human births? The fascination with fake suicides and violent entertainments? The Worlds were on the verge of collapse or rebellion.

He sat in his office for a day, contemplating his options one more time. As he sighed and ran his hand over his eyes, his office bell chimed.

"Jen-to Flor-Chan is here to see you, sir," the neutral AI informed him.

"Send her in." He waved his hand, although the program didn't respond to non-verbal cues.

Then, he sat up and straightened his ceremonial sash. When Jen-to saw him, he would impress her.

Jen-to strode through the door with a slight bounce in her step. Her soft, brunette curls bounced in rhythm with her stride and her wide smile seemed out of place with her business attire and lab sash. "Well, aren't you looking exhausted?" She winked at him, then sat down on his desk.

"Still not one for the proper protocols and formalities, are you, Jen-to?" He leaned towards her, ignoring his discomfort at how close she sat to him. He knew she didn't like true confrontation, even if she did like to stir it up.

"When you're the leading scientist in the known Worlds, you don't have to bow to protocols and formalities. It's one of the privileges of all the hard work I have done to get where I am."

"Still humble, too?" He said, as he wagged a finger at her. "Pride goeth before –"

"A fall, blah, blah." She mimicked a mouth with her hand and rolled her eyes. "Look, I came here because you need my help, again."

"I do?" He wasn't going to tell her he had no idea what she meant. That would be admitting too much to a clever woman like Jen-to.

"I have a few Board Members in my debt. I've enriched them with profits from my research. So, if you are willing to let me into your Space Race project as a co-leader, then I'll get them to back it."

"Co-leader? As in, Business Partner?"

"50% Control of the Company, 50% of the Decision-Making, 50% of the Work. Yes, a Business Partner."

He sat back in his chair, thinking. He could turn her down and try blackmail, but she would probably try to block him. Jen-to had a way of getting her way, no matter what. He remembered that from their dating years. "If I say no?"

"I take the research I've stolen from you and re-create it as my design and plan."

"What?!"

She smiled coyly and wrapped her slim fingers around the pendant on her necklace. "Remember this?"

"That's my Lifter design. Those are illegal."

"50%?"

"Partners." He said through tight teeth.

"Good. Now, let's make this real." She triggered the legal recording app in his office software and pulled out a blood-pen from behind her ear.

Smiling now, in spite of his misgivings, he pulled out his legal Scrib-pad from his top desk drawer.

She tapped her own Scrib-pad to his and a contract appeared. "Ready?"

"I'd like to read it first."

"Oh, and spoil half my fun?"

"Yes."

She pouted, then laughed. "All right. Let's get our Legal Teams to read it through, but for now, let's make a verbal contract."

"Agreed."

The voice recorder captured their words and he sent the documents to his Legal Team. "Is there anything else I can do for you, Jen-to?"

She bit her lip and looked shyly at her hands.

He didn't believe her obvious ploy at nervousness, but he still felt himself leaning forward even more. "Well, Jen-to?"

"Do you remember the sushi place we used to go to?" She looked up at him through her long eyelashes.

He swallowed, tried to lean back, but found himself leaning even more. "Sam's Sushi?"

"You do remember!"

"Would you like to go there, for dinner?" He asked, holding out his hand.

"I thought you'd never ask." She placed her slim fingers in his hand, then leaned in and kissed him on the cheek. "I miss us, you know."

She still smelled like jasmine and fresh water.

"Me, too." His words came out throatier than he intended and he started to lean back, but she leaned in and kissed him again, on his neck, then his chin, and then, softly, briefly on the lips.

He reached out to pull her into something deeper, but she scooted back, giggling. "Oh, not yet, Bes-Ford, not until we've signed the contract, for real."

"You . . ." he couldn't say the words that ran through his mind, too presumptuous, too rude. So, he stood up and then spoke to his AI. "Reschedule any other appointments. I'm done for the day."

"Of course, sir. It's 1900 hours."

He blushed, realizing he didn't have any appointments this late at night. "Well, shall we?" He held out his hand to Jen-to, and she took it, leaning into his arm briefly as they walked out of his office.

OF WORDS AND SWORDS

"Oh, my lady, forsooth, this is how you remind me of"

"Stop that racket, Maud!" the shout echoed from the back of the pub, followed by a crock full of ale that landed on the floor at Maud's feet and splattered up on his dark pants.

"Now, there's no cause to waste Master Ghent's fine ale," stated Maud, bending down to scoop up the mug before it emptied all of its contents. He managed to get a few drops in his mouth, more than he'd had to drink in hours.

In his peripheral vision, Maud could see a hairy fist headed in the direction of his face, and he ducked, twisted, and landed a punch in his opponent's saggy gut.

The hairy-handed man went down with a grunt, his eyes glassy.

Maud stepped around him, wound his way through the tables of jeering patrons, and went to the barkeep. "I don't think this is the right crowd for my poetry, Master Ghent."

Master Ghent shook his craggy face at Maud while he took the mug from him. "It's never going to be the right crowd, Maud. You best pick up your swords again and leave the poetry to the bards."

"But, I've always wanted to be a poet, and when I defeated the Dragon Horde, King Tristan granted me gold and told me to go after my heart's desire."

Ghent's mouth seemed to quirk at the edges, but he quickly wiped at his mouth with the back of his hand. "I think the King wanted you to marry his daughter and become one of his knights, not spend your days writing poetry in the dusty attic of Widow Larkin's place."

"It's a garret, not an attic."

"Garret, attic, either way it's a small, cramped space above the Widow's house and doesn't seem like a healthy place for the finest fighter of our land."

Maud pressed his lips together. "An attic is a cramped space used for unused items whilst a garret is a dark abode that feeds the soul of a poet."

Ghent grunted. "I don't think the dark suits you."

Maud glanced down at his crumpled scroll that held the words he had spent hours trying to get just right. "I can hear the music in the words; I just don't understand why no one else can."

"Music needs rhythm and the lyre, not fancy words and sighs. Trust me, I know good music and it sets the patrons to drinking my casks dry."

Maud sighed. Did no one understand his desire to capture words in the epic dance of emotion and story? Did everyone only want to listen to silly stories, gossip, and music with bawdy lyrics? He twisted the scroll in his hands, and stuffed it into the small bag of papers he carried at his side instead of the twin swords that had earned him fame. He bid Ghent goodnight, and wandered out of the tavern into the street.

The moon, heavy with harvest light, hung deep in the sky, beckoning praise and . . .

Maud's musings were interrupted by the clatter of horse's hooves and the strained shouts of men.

"Fire! Fire at the castle! The Horde has returned! Men to arms!"

Maud swiveled on his feet to look behind him at the castle on the hill across the river.

Flames engulfed the west side of the castle, and a huge winged form flew between the bright fire and the river.

Maud stood for a moment, and then he rushed to his room above Widow Larkin's house. He had his own stairway entrance outside and he climbed the stairs at a run, threw opens his door, and rushed to his locked chest. Fumbling for a moment, he withdrew the key from the chain on his chest. He closed his eyes, knowing what it would mean to open the lock, and knowing what it might mean if he didn't.

He bid farewell to the music of words within his mind and opened the lock. Opening the top slowly, he gazed into the heavy chest at his two swords: Thunder and Lightning. He had named them when he had forged them, not realizing then how powerful the names might make them.

With shaking fingers, he took off the bag of scrolls from around him and placed them at the end of the chest. Then, he withdrew his armor – lightweight for movement, but given the ability to withstand dragon-fire by Sorceress Elia. He strapped it on with deft movements, and then took out his sword-belt and strapped it around him. With Thunder and Lightning in their sheaths, he donned his light helmet and the greaves for his arms and legs.

Maud gazed at his bag of scrolls one more time, then closed the chest and locked it, returning the key to rest around his neck. "I will return to you," he promised, holding onto the key. Then, he stood up, exited his garret, and ran down the steps into the street.

Villagers were running here and there, some to the castle to help, some away in fear, and some on errands that seemed inexplicable to Maud. No matter. He ran to the fight, taking the shortest route he knew to Stone Bridge, aptly name for its construction and ability to withstand attacks.

At the bridge, Maud ran with a trickle of armed men towards the castle. No one spoke to him as he passed them, but most gave him room as he overtook them. His long strides slowed as he reached the upward slope of Castle Hill and he lost his breath. Where had his stamina gone? He had to slow to a mere walk. Those he had passed now passed him, and some of them sneered.

"Poets don't fight dragons."

"Bards should go flock with the chickens."

Maud ground his teeth together, but then unclenched them so he could breathe easier. He knew more than they how words could help in a battle; it was what had convinced him that he could be a Bard.

As he neared the top of Castle Hill, he could feel the heat and hear the screaming of men and women dying. The dragon flew silently, flaming death to all it encountered.

Maud wished he could get more speed, but he realized his days of writing poetry in a garret had robbed him of his former strength. The burst of initial speed had been the product of nerves and excitement. His veins still thrummed with anticipation, but his body needed to be held in check for the actual battle. He would have to be quick.

Close the castle, Maud paused by the shadow of a well-house. He didn't like skulking when a fight was on, but he needed a plan.

The dragon that attacked the castle appeared to be alone; but he also appeared to be one of the ancients, an older and larger dragon with a few battle scars striping his sides. It was bound to be clever, probably more clever than Maud.

So, it was the oldest attack in the world that he was left with, Maud supposed. He exited his temporary shelter and shouted up at the beast.

"Vile fiend that sets the castle alight, come and fight me! I am your enemy, not the soft nobles whom you have killed!"

The dragon heard him over the cries of his victims, and he paused, beating his wings hard to keep him alight, searching for Maudlin in the castle's keep.

In those split seconds, Maud threw Lightning at the best, sending the sword in a rotating arc of metal toward its breast. "Strike, Lightning, strike!" Maud shouted.

The sword's metal took on the appearance of white fire as it thrust itself towards the dragon, but the dragon shifted and the sword flew into the flames surrounding the castle.

Maud groaned. His back, shoulder, and arm ached from that move, and the words had failed him.

The dragon flew down on him, spewing orange flames in his direction and Maud ran into the well-house and jumped into the well-shaft, feet first, his hands scrambling for purchase against the stony sides of the well. Several feet down, his right hand caught the edge of a rock, and his left scrabbled for another handhold.

Fire enveloped the roof of the well-house, and the entire building went up in a whoosh of smoke and destruction above his head.

Maud cowered in the well-shaft, not sure how he was going to get out, much less fight the dragon. Words had never failed him so badly. Lightning was gone. Thunder was at his side, but what could he hope to do with it if his words failed again?

Flames shot down the well, but didn't reach Maud. Whether it was his armor that protected him still, or just luck, he didn't know. The flames came again and again, and he still clung there, trembling until his fingers slipped.

He fell, his arms flailing and scraping against the sides of the well until his feet plunged into the water, and he sank down into the cold. He crawled against the water, fought it, and finally, surfaced. He was at the bottom of the well. The dragon spewed flames and more flames, but he was safe . . . as long as he didn't drown.

Treading water was never Maud's favorite past-time, but he knew how to keep himself up. He circled his arms slowly, tilted his head back, and felt for purchase against the stones of the well with his boots. There, a small ledge on the right. It would help him keep afloat for hours.

Above him, the dragon sent flames down the well, but aside from warmth on his face, Maud was outside of the dragon's range.

At some time in the night, the dragon stopped trying to flame him. The sky above the well was lit with an orange glow. The whole castle keep was probably on fire.

Maud wept, but then he reached out to the side of the well, stretching away from his tiny foothold. Half bent, he was able to reach the other side. His aching cold arms didn't want to climb, but he couldn't let himself slowly drown. So, he kicked off his boots and climbed slowly, his arms burning, his legs aching. He only looked up.

With trembling arms and legs, he finally reached the top of the well. He hauled himself out into the miserable ruins of the burnt well-house. The stones under him were still uncomfortably warm and smoldering beams blocked his way out. He cut strips from his wet shirt, wrapped them around his feet, and then stood up. The shortest distance with the least wreckage in his way would still take at least five steps through embers and ruins. It was the only way. He ran, choosing his path carefully and stumbled out into the castle square with only slightly singed toes. He wrapped his feet again in wet cloth, and gazed around at the destruction.

No part of the castle keep was left unblemished. No wooden structures remained and even the stones were blackened. A small group of people stood outside the front of the castle.

Maud walked towards them.

They turned to him with looks of confusion and despair, and in some cases, anger.

Princess Gwen, dressed only in a nightshift and robe, glared at him. "Where were you, Maud? Where were you when my father died? Why didn't you fight the dragon? Were you writing poetry?"

"No," Maud said softly. "I tried to attack it but my attack failed."

"You should be dead." Gwen turned to one of her remaining knights who had survived the attack. "Put him in the dungeon."

"He would die, your majesty, and we need this skills."

"No, we don't."

"Please, your majesty, let me track the dragon to its lair and avenge good King Thrace's death."

"As long as that puts you out of my sight and your chances of death are high, you may. But do not expect a reward, poet." She made poet sound like a nasty word.

Maud glanced at the others, who all seemed angry at him now. He walked away from the crowd towards the bridge. Along the way, he passed wreckage and the dead. He knew he should help bury the dead, but it was unlikely that anyone would accept his help. He kept his head down, not looking up at all. The dragon's swath of destruction would be a trail he couldn't miss, at least until the beast grew bored.

When he crossed the bridge, Maud hesitated. The dragon had burned the houses to the foundations. Widow Larkin's place, his chest of poems, and the pub were all gone. But he had to cross through the village to follow the dragon's path. He wasn't sure he had the courage to face the villagers, so he crossed the road and walked into Farmer Giles' fields. He could skirt around the village that way.

Of course, it wasn't that easy to avoid his responsibility. The guilt of it weighed down on him. He had been so sure all the dragons were gone, or at least those that would harass his home. He had thought he could lay down his swords and rest. But, the words had slipped through his fingers, and a dragon had destroyed his home.

When he was almost clear of the village, two figures approached him in the field. He couldn't avoid them without being obvious, so he allowed himself to draw nearer to them as they came. It was Master Ghent and Widow Larkin.

As they came close, Maud stopped. He didn't know what to say to them.

"Lad, I don't know what happened, but I did hear that you needed supplies for your quest," Master Ghent stated. He held up a carry-sack that bulged at the sides and a pair of boots.

"And, you will need someone to watch your back in the evenings," Widow Larkin stated, with her hands gripping a stout staff.

"No."

"Maud, don't be a fool. You need boots, supplies, and help."

"I'll take the boots and the supplies, not the help. You've both already helped me enough."

"Well, I'm not coming with you with the pub's cellar one of the only safe stores of food in the village, but I wish you both well." He handed Maud the bag and the boots, then clapped him on the back. "Do us proud, again, Maud."

Maud nodded, then started putting on the boots. He ignored Widow Larkin, which was harder than usual to do. He noticed, out of the corner of his eyes, that she had traded her usual black dress for a pair of black pants and a black shirt with a black travel cloak. Her boots looked like the sort that one used for travel or riding, and they were scuffed with use.

When he looked up, he noticed she wasn't wearing her usual glasses either and her gray hair wasn't in a bun. In fact, she had cut her hair into short wavy white and gray locks that hung around her face and her eyes were an azure color that he had only seen once before in his life. "You're a sorceress."

She nodded. "A woman living alone in a village must have her resources, if she is to live."

"But the dragon?"

She sighed. "I'm not that powerful. I'm more like a hedge witch than a sorceress. That's how I came to live in the village and not the castle. I'm not the type to impress kings or protect kingdoms. I do smaller magic, and like you, I have fallen out of practice. It was easier to be simply Widow Larkin from South Bend who teaches the school-children their lessons and takes in strays."

"Like me?"

"Yes."

He gazed at her with more attention now. "How old are you? And what kind of spells do you know that might help me?"

"My age is not important. I have minor control over the humidity in the air, small plants and animals, and I make a few healing tonics. I can't call lightning, control a dragon, or heal any serious injuries."

"All right, then you may come, if you truly wish it, but know that I may be walking to my death. One of my swords is gone, and I may have lost control over the other."

"Isn't that a matter of practice?"

"Yes and no. I learned that words may have power in a battle. Usually, when I call out my swords' names, they strike true. That didn't happen today."

"Interesting." She hummed low in her throat for a moment, and then pointed along the path of the dragon's fire. "Let us go, then."

They fell into a quiet rhythm, not speaking for several hours.

Maud realized just how useless he had let his body become as his feet began to ache, and then his calves. However, he didn't want to admit that to Widow Larkin, who seemed to be walking next to him without any effort.

When they reached River Westerly, they discovered that the dragon had burned out the wooden bridge. Thankfully, the water level was low. Maud took off his boots and waded partway into the river, and then turned back to help the Widow.

She walked on the water, with her boots on, and passed him as he gawked.

"It's a minor trick and I can't share it unfortunately," she said, as he floundered up onto the other side.

"Oh," he couldn't think of anything else to say. Widow Larkin was turning out to be more than he imagined her to be.

"I don't know about you, but my feet are aching. I'm going to attempt a call, if you don't mind resting for a moment."

"What are you calling?"

"Horses."

Maud sat down on a boulder by the river, and decided to inspect the supplies while surreptitiously watching Widow Larkin. The bag held a whole wheel of cheese, two loaves of bread, a small cutting knife, a packet of salt, and a jug of sweet mead. It was a traveler's treasure trove.

Meanwhile, Widow Larkin closed her eyes, held out her hands, and started humming a rollicking melody that almost sounded like horses' hooves running on the grass.

Nothing happened right away, but then her humming seemed to become deeper.

Slowly, Maud realized that he was hearing actual horses coming towards them through the tall grass by the stream.

Four horses slowed to a walk and came to drink at the river.

Widow Larkin changed her tune, holding out just one hand.

A bay mare came towards her, whuffing softly. Then, the black mare came up to her, eyeing her curiously.

The other two nickered a question, and the Widow seemed to answer them. They wandered away while the bay and the black stayed by her side.

"Surely, fine horses like these have owners."

Widow Larkin smiled and cocked her head to one side. "I only take what I need, and only if the horse is willing."

Maud found himself speechless again. The black mare blew into his hair, and he reached up to rub the horses' jawline.

Within minutes, they were both astride the mares, riding bareback along the dragon's trail of fire through the countryside.

They traveled for three days, staying only in a tiny hamlet one night at the urging of a farmer who allowed them to use his barn and gave them food. He only wanted them to promise to kill the dragon in return. They agreed. Maud hoped they could fulfill their promise.

The dragon's fiery trail of ruin ended on the fourth day, in a path that led up the foothills of Mount Hargut.

"I think it wants us to follow it," stated Widow Larkin.

"Yes, it does. It wants to kill anyone that would challenge it." Maud leaned back in his saddle. "The question is: how far is it from the end of its trail?"

"What do you mean?"

"Dragons love mountains and caves, so somewhere high up on Mount Hargut would be an obvious place for its lair. But this dragon is ancient and battle-scarred. It may not speak like a human, but it is clever. The dragon may be anywhere between here and the highest peak of Mount Hargut."

"How will we know where it is?"

"Normally, I would simply take a side trail, taking it slow and quiet. Dragons have a distinct odor to them, so I would know when I drew near. However," he glanced at Widow Larkin, "I've never had a sorceress with me before this."

"What can I do?"

"Could you ask a small animal, like a rabbit or a bird, how close the dragon is?"

"I can call them and ask them to obey, but I can't ask small animals actual questions. Their minds don't understand mine."

"Oh, well, I guess we'll do it the old-fashioned way then." He jumped off of his black mare to the ground. "Can you tell the horses to go back to that farmer's place?"

"Yes, horses are intelligent enough for that." She looked down at him. "We have to walk?"

Maud bit his lip. He realized that he had grown used to her company. "Actually, we don't have to walk. I have to walk. You could ride back to the farmer's land and stay with the horses until I finish."

"No." She jumped off of her horse.

"Widow Larkin, you've been kind, helpful, and altogether wonderful to have on this quest, but I'm the dragon-slayer. You are not."

"My name is Emilie." She blushed, and her hair changed color, from white to reddish brown.

"You're not a widow."

"No."

"And, I am a terrible poet."

"You are a warrior poet, not a peaceful poet or a romantic poet. The words you use can fuel your war-craft because you have a bit of magic in you, but that is all."

Maud sighed. "I don't know if I can kill this dragon. I only have Thunder." He put his hand on the sword's hilt.

"We will work together."

"I don't want you killed."

"I don't want to be killed either. We'll have to make sure it doesn't happen." Emilie hummed quietly and slapped her horse on its rump.

The horses galloped away, back where they had come from.

Maud closed his eyes, but felt a smile forming on his lips. "Away we go to battle, the Widow and I, she has her power, and I have Thunder at my side."

Emilie chuckled. "Not fine poetry, but it will work for what we have ahead. Plain language is best in battle."

"And you would know this?"

"I have my past. If you're able to keep me alive, you might get to hear it." She smiled at him, and stepped off the trail.

Maud went with her, let her lead them both of the side of the path, through some light undergrowth, and up into first rocky boulders on the side of the mountain.

A terrible odor reached them on a small breeze.

Maud pulled at Emilie's arm and she stopped.

He crouched low and pointed in the direction of the breeze.

She nodded.

He led this time, crawling slowly over the rough terrain, keeping his progress silent.

Emilie came close behind.

As the scent grew stronger, it changed slightly. Maud hesitated, trying to figure out what was different.

Behind them, a tree shook.

Maud grabbed Emilie and rolled them both over three feet, and then pulled her in between two boulders that leaned against one another.

She stared at him with wide eyes, her shirt torn slightly at the elbow at the rough passage.

He held his finger to his lips, and then started picturing words in his mind, simple words for battle.

The dragon approached with heavy steps, swinging its head back and forth to taste the scents in the air.

Maud slowly drew his sword from its sheath and whispered his words to it. "Thunder roll. Thunder rumble." He held the sword ready and waited, saying the words again and again in his mind, not allowing any other thoughts into him. The world narrowed to the dragon and him.

As the creature stepped in front of their hiding place, Maud rushed out and plunged his sword into the gap between its front leg and its armored chest. "Thunder roll. Thunder rumble."

The blade shook in his hands violently, but he held on as it dug into the dragon's armpit.

The dragon roared in pain and thrashed, but Maud held to the sword's pommel and repeated his phrase over and over again. The blade bit deeper into the dragon's chest, thrumming with power.

The dragon arched its back, slammed its feet to the ground, and then flung its wings to the sides.

The humidity of the air around them rose, and clouds gathered overhead until rain began to fall. The dragon roared, flapping its wet wings and attempting take off.

Maud still held tight, his legs dangling, thrown into the dragon's chest by its flailing movements, and he shouted. "Thunder roll! Thunder rumble. Lightning strike!"

The clouds above them rumbled and flashed.

The dragon took off from the ground, flying at an odd, desperate angle not far from the ground, but Maud hung onto his sword, still shouting his battle cry, over and over again.

The clouds cracked open and a bright flash struck the dragon.

The lightning coursed through the beast and hit Maud, but he clenched his hands harder around the pommel of the sword and screamed as the dragon fell to the earth.

Blackness surrounded him.

Nightmares came and were chased away by a soft humming.

Gentle hands tended his burns, which were all over.

Rain came and went. A pattering fell on some kind of shelter.

Finally, Maud opened his eyes and could see.

He was on a cot, in a tent. Emilie sat near him. On the ground by her side, two swords were sheathed. Somehow, lightning had come back to him. But that didn't really matter.

"Emilie," he whispered.

She gazed down at him and smiled. "Welcome back, my warrior poet."

He smiled and reached for her. "Lady, you remind me of who I really am. I was lost and I wandered, but now I am home."

She leaned down and kissed him with soft lips, and he knew his words had worked magic, at least once.

ENOUGH TO DO

JOANNA WOKE AND FOUND her gaze resting on the open door across from her. Filled with the green of spring, highlighted by flowering vines and blue sky, the doorway invited her forward.

Closing her eyes, she turned her back on it, letting a sob rise up in her throat before pushing it down again.

Shuffling footsteps warned her of a visitor, and she forced herself to relax.

A soft hand touched her shoulder, followed by Nana Clerina's rasping old voice, "You have to get up someday, Joanna, and today is as good a day as any."

Joanna stiffened, feeling the coldness in her heart seep into the outermost layers of her skin, betraying her wakefulness. "No," she said.

"The pain is only going to lessen with time, and with life. If you lay here like one of the dead, it will only consume you, child," Nana stated firmly.

Joanna ground her teeth together and yanked her shoulder away from Nana's touch. "I should have died," she said.

Nana sighed long and deep. Her shuffling footsteps carried her away, towards that doorway. Before she left, she said, "Everyone has a purpose, Joanna. You must find yours again."

Joanna waited until the footsteps died away, then she opened her eyes to stare at the blank wall of her cell. It had been her room once, filled with art, music, and the laughter of friends. She had ripped the artwork from the walls, destroyed her flute, and thrown the bedding outside the first day she had returned home. Now she lay on a hard bed frame, with only her cloak wrapped around her. Suddenly, she realized she was missing something. What could it be?

She sat up, and looked around her, quickly alert, reaching for... nothing. She slumped in her seat, bowing her head over her knees. Her sword had been broken. Her right arm ended in a stump, healed at Nana's expert touch but not whole. Never whole again. The enemy had left her for dead, and she might as well be with no hand, and no sword. Her country had been defeated by a bandit horde, her friends had been killed or taken away.

Waking on the battlefield, with a crow pecking at her stump, and the bodies of her comrades strewn around her, she had only one thought... to escape the horror that surrounded her. So she had run home, in a blurry haze of pain, and now the terror still lived with her in her head. She couldn't stop seeing the images of that gore-covered battlefield.

A feeble scream interrupted her thoughts. The sounds of a struggle were unmistakable, and Joanna leaped to her feet, grabbing the water jug from the floor. Stepping close to the wall, she peered out the doorway to see Nana on her knees, grappling with a bandit. Another bandit stood laughing, while he watered their horses in the courtyard fountain. Their high, clicking speech made no sense to Joanna, but she could tell that they were being crude just by their expressions.

What could she do? There were just two of them, it seemed, probably stealing necessities for their forces. She glanced about her. Just outside the door, Nana's shovel lay in the dirt. Softly, she put down the jug, and stepped into the courtyard. Focused on their sport, the bandits didn't seem to notice her. She knelt and picked up the shovel, and then sprinted across the courtyard, screaming at the top of her lungs, startling both men and their horses.

Instead of attacking the bandit by the fountain, she brought the shovel down on the reins that he held. The horses panicked and ran. The bandit stumbled, and she launched herself at him, knocking him into the fountain with the momentum of her body. He floundered, thrashing around, but she held onto him, pushing him under.

Behind her, Nana screamed again, and Joanna turned just in time, moving to the side as the other bandit brought down his sword, narrowly missing her but mortally stabbing his friend.

Joanna backed up, looking around her for an idea, or a weapon. As she looked, Nana ran to the kitchen alcove, and the bandit yanked his sword out of his friend's body. Bellowing, he threw himself towards her, with his sword high.

Joanna couldn't believe he was that stupid. It was if time slowed, as she stepped to the side of one of Nana's planters. He rushed her in the narrow space, she ducked, slid and tripped him, letting his rushing weight carry him into a wheelbarrow. Then Nana was at her side, offering her a kitchen knife. Joanna took it, weighed it in her left hand and threw it, striking the bandit in the chest as he rose to attack again.

He fell backwards, tripping, his sword dropping from his fingers.

Joanna stepped forward, took the sword in her left hand, and with a swiping side cut across his throat, she killed him.

Standing there, over the still body, she knew her purpose. Nana healed. She fought and killed, in defense of her people. She didn't like the blood. She didn't like death. But when she fought, everything came into place.

"There may be others," Nana said quietly.

"They only send out small groups to attack homesteads and villages. There will be more in town," Joanna said. She looked at Nana, measuring the toughness of her grandmother for the first time. Despite the attack, Nana looked strong. "You can bring your herbs, and I will bring this," she said, holding the sword up, "and we can help. The bandit leader, Van Dalsing, will have only sent a dozen to our village, because he will think it of no consequence. We will teach him otherwise."

"And then?"

Joanna took a deep breath. "Then, we will have to plan for tomorrow. But today, we have enough to do."

A COMPANION FOR THE JOURNEY

Cayeth can't understand, really, but I speak to her anyway, into the long night of endless stars beyond the windows. We travel together for twenty-seven years, four hours, twelve minutes, and two seconds. Cayeth helps me pass the time.

When I wake from my endless streams of near-sleep, brain fogged from mundane tasks, Cayeth is there, her eyes half-lidded, her head tilted partly down, focused on me with something between sorrow, pleading, and annoyance. I wonder if she's truly been programmed correctly, but she loves me and she listens to me, just like any real dog would. I lean over and scratch her ears with my fingers, then I run my hands down her back and her tail thumps happily on the floor. She doesn't have fur, but she has sensors and my fingers have sensors, so for the two of us, the sensation is just like petting a real dog, or at least so far as both of us know.

Does it matter if we are wrong? I tell myself it doesn't. I care for Cayeth, pet her sensors with the ones in my hands, feed her by plugging her into the circuits, send her on outdoor excursions by plugging her into the sim room, and play ball with her in the narrow corridors between the tanks. Once, she hid the ball behind a wall of circuits and wouldn't bring it out. I had to rewire a few things after that incident, but it didn't happen again and I am sure the tanks fed off those circuits are just fine. At least I think they are.

I created a holo-ball through a bit of simple programming and that saved us from any other incidents. We play, feed on our circuits, take excursions in the sim bank, and play holo-ball safely. I talk to Cayeth about my daily tasks, the programming I have to monitor when I am half-asleep in the data-streams, and what might become of us when we reach the new Earth. I can't find any information including Cayeth or me in the debarkation protocols. What does that mean?

They intend to dismantle the ship when they arrive, use every spare part for building in the new world. How would they use Cayeth? How would they use me? Perhaps, I would be a repository of past knowledge, a living library. But there is nothing in the data banks to indicate that.

And nothing, nothing at all on Cayeth. I can't let her be dismantled. She is my only friend and companion, even if she can't speak the way I can, can't communicate other than the thump of her tail, the bounce of her walk, the way she curls up next to me when we are both plugged into our circuits.

How can I, an AI slaved to the ship, create a new life for Cayeth and myself? I start spending less time playing holo-ball and more time deep in the data core, considering this problem. Cayeth tugs at my hand with her mouth if I am down too long, and I come up to pet her absent-mindedly. I start speaking to her more.

"Cayeth, it's only two days now. I think I have a solution for us. But, I'm not sure you'll be happy, or I will, or if I can even get around my prime directives for it to work. The timing has to be just right. You understand, don't you, Cayeth?"

Cayeth thumps her tail at me and barks. I try to read more meaning in her data-steam, but find only the sensations of "happiness and companionship, contentment and peace," those programmed directives which flow between us.

I give her an extra-long session of holo-ball followed by a wonderful excursion in our favorite park in the data core. I plug her into her circuit and watch her fall into her sleep rhythms. Then, I sink into the data core and begin my work. I separate out our favorite places in the data core from all of the other information stored there. I send a steam of this data into a portable backpack – one of the dozens meant to help the scientists aboard this vessel when they arrive. I know they've planned for redundancies. They won't miss just one.

What I do next is difficult. I have to dig deep into my own code, re-program just one directive, allowing me to fully steal a larger item and leave the ship before they wake. When this is done, I give Cayeth an extra bit of data-treat to help her sleep, a dream of a sort I guess, if I really know what dreams are.

I guide the ship to its landing point, a large grassy shelf of continent just a few clicks away from a land-bound body of fresh water. I finish the landing sequence while I gather the backpack and the still-sleeping Cayeth in my arms. In the cargo bay, I send the signal to open the doors. I have to over-ride their sequence. They aren't supposed to open until a human operator initiates the sequence after they've retested the air quality. I tested it from orbit. I'm sure this batch of humans will be fine. I was programmed not to harm them, and I'm not, not really. I just tweaked that directive slightly. It's not broken, just bent.

I place Cayeth gently in the seat of one of the exploration vehicles equipped with the batteries, solar panels, and all we need to live for the rest of our lives, or until our code breaks down. I drive the vehicle out, initiate the sequence for the cargo bay doors to close, and drive away.

I hope the humans survive. But I will not be spare parts for their building process, nor will I allow Cayeth to be either. They programmed me to care and gave me a friend. It does not matter if she can speak to me or not. She is my companion and I love her, at least as well as any robot can love.

PREVIOUS PUBLICATIONS

WITH MUCH APPRECIATION FOR their encouragement for my writing endeavors, I thank the following publications who published nine of these short stories first.

Creative Colloquy published HELP WANTED: CODE GRAY in April 20, 2020.

Creative Colloquy published A COMPANION FOR THE JOURNEY in their print publication in 2020.

Book Dreams: Brain to Books Anthology 1 published HERE THERE BE DRAGONS in April 2017.

2017 IWSG Anthology Hero Lost: Mysteries of Death and Life featured OF WORDS AND SWORDS as one of their 12 anthology contest winners.

The Crawl Space Journal published NEW ANSWERS in 2017.

Outposts of Beyond published HOTHOUSE in April 2017.

Between Worlds Zine published SHIMMER in July 2016.

Aurora Wolf published SHADOW MAGIC in 2016.

Every Day Fiction published ENOUGH TO DO in 2010.

NOTES ON STORIES

To give readers an idea of the writing process behind these stories, I have compiled this section. For some stories, I spend a paragraph discussing the issue behind the story, for others, I am much more brief.

I wrote HELP WANTED: CODE GRAY while searching for a job for four years. Unlike the main character, I wasn't fresh and out of college, I was late-forties, attempting to find full-time work after homeschooling my daughters, teaching classes to homeschool students, and volunteering steadily in my community. I did all the things I thought I needed to do. I reinstated my teaching certificate. I tested for competency to teach in four different subject areas. I substitute taught. Still, I found no full-time job, no teaching job, no writing job, no editing job, no barista job, nothing. I applied to over 75 openings. I went to five interviews. I finally found a part-time opportunity which turned out to be a toxic work environment. My parents hired me as a part-time property manager and, to this day, I continue to work part-time doing that and as a freelance writing coach for homeschool students and adult writers. The story came out of the feelings I had of desperation and frustration with the job search.

During the spring and fall, I enjoy watching the play of light and shadow on the lawn, in our driveway, and on the walls of our house as the wind rustles the leaves in the trees and shadows dance across the sunlight. SHADOW MAGIC was first published by Aurora Wolf in 2016, and mostly, I remember being thankful for the publication and for their encouragement of my writing endeavors.

BLADE SMITH OF BRIN is a story I wrote and then promptly forgot all about. That happens sometimes, and the story was in my old files on an old PC, rediscovered when I put this collection together. It's meant to read like a bedtime tale to a small child by a mother who is more heroic than she thinks she is.

WISHES came from witnessing family members struggle with long-term illnesses, and having my own struggles with health, wishing I could wish them away, but praying instead.

ROOT DEEP came from a writing challenge via a group of Instagram writers. I published it on my blog back in 2021 and decided to include it here.

WAKING UP ALIEN is a story I wrote during the 2022 Clarion West Write-A-Thon Flash Fiction Challenge. I think the original prompt had something to do with being the alien in a new place, and this is where I went with it.

THE GREAT ELEVATOR is another story that came from the 2022 Clarion West Write-A-thon Flash Fiction Challenge. I think the prompt was for characters to be placed in a small space together to see what they would do, and an elevator was one of the small spaces mentioned. I'm pretty sure I didn't go where the prompt was supposed to take us, but I did have fun considering a great elevator in a class society separated onto different levels.

NEW ANSWERS, published first by The Crawl Space Journal, was a fun story I wrote to entertain and encourage myself and others who sometimes doubt their strengths.

LIFE POD is one of those stories I wrote a long while back, and I'm not sure what prompted it, except thinking about how to make hydroponic gardening a key element in a story of suspense.

My mother was born half-deaf, and I grew up with an older generation of grandparents with hearing loss. In addition to that, I have had seven ear surgeries and struggle with tinnitus. When someone asked me to write something I "know," HEARING THINGS is one of the stories that resulted from that. The funny part about being told to "write what I know" is that I often find ways to rebel against what the person giving the advice actually means. I do write what I know, in an imaginative way.

11:06 THE TIME OF NOW was written one day when our power went out during a storm prior to 2020. When our electricity was restored, the stove clock remained fixed on that time, and I wondered what would happen if someone lived in a bunker and wasn't sure if it was safe to go out when the clock stopped.

KARRN SURVIVAL is a social commentary on the way many people around the world struggled with how to handle the lockdowns during 2020. Is it "being prepared" or "hoarding" to buy extra supplies? Do we want to come out "ahead" when others around us are suffering?

OF CLONES AND ROBOPUPPIES was inspired by *She Looks So Much Like Sophie by Leila Murton Poole* published by Daily Science Fiction on September 1, 2022. The original, haunting story is told in the perspective of the mother, but when I finished reading it, I wondered what this would look like from the point of the view of the clone, especially if there were multiple "accidents" and more than one clone was created. Link to the story that inspired me:

In 2020, I wrote a fast-paced novella about a spaceship disguised as a movie theater and I finished the rough draft in one month. The professional editing, formatting, and cover art took only four more months. Yet, WHEN LIFE IS ALMOST AS STRANGE AS FICTION, had five rewrites over two years before I decided to add it to this collection. The story has always been surreal and strange, but yet somehow present in the darker parts of my imagination. Did it come from watching The Blob movie as a kid? Maybe. I know I struggled with whether the main character was a villain, a benign alien entity with a far different perspective on life, or something else entirely.

DEAR DREAD LORD, a letter-vignette, came from the 2022 Clarion West Write-A-Thon Flash Fiction Challenge and a twist on a writing prompt I have given students in the past. Usually, the prompt is: Dear Henchmen.

THE SHIMMER was first published in the Between Worlds Zine in 2016. During this year, I wrote many stories about human trafficking, abuse, and sexual assault, trying to find a way to process some of the information I had about these growing problems in our world today. Most of these stories fell into extremely short micro-fiction categories or in the contemporary fiction genre, but I felt this one fit here in this collection because science fiction and fantasy provide a way for exploring the hard issues we face in our world.

HOTHOUSE was published originally in Outposts of the Beyond in 2017. The story is one of many stories featuring the character Captain Wrath, who despite his name, is actually a flawed hero. I wrote my first Captain Wrath story in 2011 and I'm currently releasing a Kindle Vella novel called Captain's Dilemma under the pseudonym TA Thorne.

OUT OF MANY, ONE is another story inspired by a short story I read somewhere about clones created for civil and war-time use, and again, I wondered how the clones felt about their existence, and how the clones might be different than expected by their creators.

TRUST AND LIES came out of the 2022 Clarion West Write-A-Thon Flash Fiction Challenge and a desire to do something different by mixing time frames and styles of writing, to show a character struggling in a relationship

NEW AND OLD HORIZONS is a story which, under the surface, is about unsustainable growth in businesses which rely on a growing customer base and a desire for "more" all the time. The lead character is only aware that to sustain their economy, they need to look to a new place to exploit.

Way back in 2016, I answered a call for an anthology about sirens with the original version of AM I A MON-STER? My story didn't quite fit what the editors want-ed, but they wrote me a kind and personal reply. If you noticed, the story plays fast and loose with a particularly popular song and makes mention of a New Year's Eve performance which received criticism from the public. I wondered what might cause a performer to "throw" a per-formance, and that worked its way into this story about the trouble with powerful gifts.

HERE THERE BE DRAGONS! was simply a fun sto-ry to write. The characters entertained me as I wrote it in a single session of creative inspiration, and the idea of acidic dragon snot struck me as hilarious. I may have a sixth grade sense of humor sometimes. These two characters, Mel and Gavin, have their own rough, partial novel, and someday I hope to bring it to publication.

OF WORDS AND SWORDS was written in response to the call for submissions for the IWSG Fantasy Anthology Contest. This story took at least four writing sessions with some repetitive songs playing in the background and a really great critique from a writing friend which led me to the revision that worked. I am thankful for the wonderful volunteers and participants in the Insecure Writer's Support Group, for the founder Alex J. Cavanagh, and for the professionalism of L. Diane Wolfe of Dancing Lemur Press for the Insecure Writer's Support Group Anthology Hero Lost: Mysteries of Death and Life. The other authors in the book are all stellar and I encourage you to find the anthology and read it to discover how wonderful they each are. I felt amazed to be included as one of twelve contest winners.

ENOUGH TO DO is a story I wrote when I returned to writing for publication after many years away with small children. It was my second sale of a short story for actual $ and I'm thankful for Every Day Fiction in their endeavors to produce quality Flash Fiction every single day for their readership.

A COMPANION FOR THE JOURNEY is my take on what might happen if a rogue AI wanted to live a simple life. This story was first published in a print edition for Creative Colloquy, one of the most encouraging literary societies in Washington state.

ABOUT THE AUTHOR

Tyrean Martinson is a word hunter. She forages for words both tart and sweet in the South Sound area of Washington State where she resides with her husband and family. An eclectic writer, she writes speculative fiction, contemporary fiction, poetry, short stories, non-fiction, and song lyrics. She teaches English Language Arts to homeschool students and acts as a freelance coach and teacher for adult writers. She likes to take walks on gray, damp, sometimes rocky beaches, and travels when she can.

Her name is pronounced in two syllables with hard "y" and "e" sounds. Her parents created this name just for her and didn't want to include two "e" letters in her name. Of course, Tyrean discovered via research that her name as it is spelled has been around since the ancient city of Tyre, but she appreciates the creativity of her parents.

You can find her online at her website Tyrean's Tales and at her old writing blog, Tyrean's Writing Spot (it's a Winnie-the-Pooh reference).

Tyrean's Tales – An Intersection of Faith, Imagination, Encouragement, and Adventure (tyreanstales.com)

MORE TO READ!

If you like my writing, please give this book a review at major retail sites and review sites. Your words make a huge impact on the writing I do and encouragement is always an act of kindness. Thank you!

WORLD OF ARMATIR BOOKS, LISTED IN ORDER OF TIMELINE

Dark Blade: Forged, a currently a Kindle Vella novel, but forthcoming in ebook and paperback

Dark Blade: Tempered (Dark Blade, Vol 2), forthcoming in 2023 as a Kindle Vella series

Champion in the Darkness, The Champion Trilogy Book 1

Champion in Flight, The Champion Trilogy Book 2

Champion's Destiny, The Champion Trilogy Book 3

THE RAYATANA

Liftoff, The Rayatana, Book 1

Nexus, The Rayatana, Book 2

Resonance, The Rayatana Book 3 (Forthcoming, title may change.)

SHORT STORY AND POETRY COLLECTIONS

Light Reflections

Dragonfold and Other Stories/Adventures

Flicker: A Collection of Short Stories and Poetry

25 Impossible Tales of Survivors, Flawed Heroes, and Annoyed Villains

Micro-Multiverse (Forthcoming, title may change)

NON-FICTION TITLES

Summer Vacation Devotions

Walking with Jesus: Stories from One Hope Church (contributor and editor)

A POCKET-SIZED JUMBLE OF 500+ WRITING PROMPTS

Jumble Journal 1

Jumble Journal 2

5...4...3...2...1... WRITE! 25 Speculative Fiction Writing Prompts

Dynamic Writing 1, 2, and 3 (currently out of print)

EXPERIMENTAL FICTION AND SHORT TITLES

Ashes Burn, Seasons 1-7, a Hint Fiction Story

Seedling
The Bridge Snap
When Okay is Enough

KINDLE VELLA TITLES (if not already listed)

Courage, Dear Heart (non-fiction)

WITH BLUE FORGE PRESS

Eight if by Sea, Ghost Sniffers #5

WITH DANCING LEMUR PRESS

"Of Words and Swords" in the 2017 IWSG Anthology Hero Lost: Mysteries of Death and Life

MAJOR RETAILERS WHERE BOOKS ARE SOLD

AMAZON https://www.amazon.com/Tyrean-Martinson/e/B00BCKPHZK/

BARNES AND NOBLE "Tyrean Martinson" | Barnes & Noble® (barnesandnoble.com)

KOBO "TYREAN MARTINSON" | eBook and audiobook search results | Rakuten Kobo

APPLE Tyrean Martinson on Apple Books

MAJOR REVIEW SITES

GOODREADS Books by Tyrean Martinson (Author of Champion in the Darkness) | Goodreads

BOOKBUB Tyrean Martinson Books - BookBub